"Now that Cynthia's going to be free—"

There. She'd made a start. "I'm sure you will want a divorce, too."

Drew frowned and studied her in silence. Then he said, very quietly, "Brodie, the promise I made to you was a lifelong one."

"But you said, if I wanted out—"

"I told you that I would let you go. But you can't just pretend you're doing me a good deed."

Yet if he still loved Cynthia, why had he not reached out for his freedom?

The answer was suddenly clear. If Drew were to divorce Brodie, she would be alone again, without a job or anyone to care for her. So Drew felt obliged to take care of her— while Brodie was acting out of love.

D1012245

LEIGH MICHAELS is married to "the best photographer in the United States," and in 1979 they published a photo book, *Pilgrimage*, documenting the Pope's visit to their hometown of Des Moines, Iowa. She believes all good writing is actually rewriting, and confesses to having sent a quarter of a million words up in smoke herself, but who's counting? Leigh holds a degree in journalism and teaches now and then at a community college. Her family includes two teenagers, a cross-bred mutt who thinks he's human and a Siamese "aristo-cat." Leigh loves to write and has enough ideas for romances to keep her busy for a long time.

Books by Leigh Michaels

HARLEQUIN PRESENTS
702—KISS YESTERDAY GOODBYE
811—DEADLINE FOR LOVE
835—DREAMS TO KEEP
876—TOUCH NOT MY HEART

HARLEQUIN ROMANCE
2657—ON SEPTEMBER HILL
2734—WEDNESDAY'S CHILD
2748—COME NEXT SUMMER

LEIGH MICHAELS

leaving home

Harlequin Books

TORONTO • NEW YORK • LONDON
AMSTERDAM • PARIS • SYDNEY • HAMBURG
STOCKHOLM • ATHENS • TOKYO • MILAN

Harlequin Presents first edition July 1986
ISBN 0-373-10900-8

Original hardcover edition published in 1985
by Mills & Boon Limited

CHAPTER ONE

'THERE it is! Look, Jerry. You can just see it over the treetops!' Brodie was almost bouncing in her seat as the car made a sharp turn off the highway. 'Isn't it beautiful?'

Jerry laughed. 'All this excitement over a house?' he teased. His voice was indulgent, and he didn't take his eyes off the road.

'Safe Harbour is not just any house, Jerry.' But Brodie was too excited to be irritated at him. She leaned forward, propping her elbows on the instrument panel of his old car, to get the best view of the slate roof of Safe Harbour. It was all she could see from this angle of the tall old house on the hill, and it wasn't enough to satisfy Brodie's hunger for home. 'Please hurry!'

'If we get stopped for speeding, you can explain it to the officer.'

'I haven't been home in three months. Is it any wonder that I'm looking forward to a whole summer at Safe Harbour?'

'A whole summer?' Jerry looked at her quizzically. 'You haven't changed your mind about marrying me, have you?'

The house disappeared, hidden behind a block of commercial buildings, and Brodie leaned back in her seat and turned to look at him. 'Of course not. But there's no sense in renting an apartment for a few weeks when we'll be going back to school in the fall. I'm sure Drew will want us to stay at Safe Harbour after the wedding.'

Jerry grunted. 'Well, you may be certain, but I'm not. I can't see that guardian of yours being agreeable about

5

anything, much less you getting married right now. And I'm not the best catch in town.'

Brodie laughed gaily. 'Jerry, when it comes down to it, it's really none of Drew's business. After all, I'm not a baby anymore.'

'But you are only twenty.'

'In September, he won't even be my guardian any more,' Brodie pointed out. 'As of my next birthday, I will be officially responsible for myself. He won't say no to me now. And if you want to talk about being a good catch——'

'I'm not looking forward to discussing it with Drew Hammond, no. Attorneys scare me stiff.'

'Well, lots of people start off on the wrong side of the tracks. It doesn't mean they have to stay there.'

'I don't think even you will get him to agree to that, Brodie.'

She pulled one foot up under her on the upholstered seat. 'Oh, for heaven's sake, there is no caste system in Hammond's Point.'

'Just try telling that to Drew Hammond. He thinks he still owns this town because his great-great-grandfather built it.'

'As long as you're speaking of the wrong side of the tracks, that man was the black sheep of two families back East before he came to Iowa with the wagon trains.' She bit her lip and pleaded, 'Look, Jerry, Drew has been like an uncle to me since I was five. Please don't say awful things about him.'

'Face it, Brodie, your so-called Uncle Drew is a cold, supercilious, arrogant snob.'

'He is not! You don't even know him, and of course you're scared to meet him. But you shouldn't feel inferior. You'll like Drew, really.'

Jerry didn't sound convinced. 'Tell me once more how you got mixed up with the Hammonds.'

'My father and Andy Hammond—Drew's father— were childhood friends,' Brodie recited. 'So my dad named Andy as my guardian, and when Andy died a few years later, lucky Drew inherited me right along with Safe Harbour and Andy's law practice.' The explanation had the ring of repetition, as though Brodie didn't even have to think about it. And she promptly forgot the subject entirely as the car chugged noisily up the hill and she got her first good look at Safe Harbour.

The wrought iron gates in the high brick wall stood open in welcome, and the house seemed to smile down at her from the hilltop where it reigned over the little city of Hammond's Point, nestled into a river valley. Brodie drew a breath of sheer happiness. The house was so big and so warm and so incredibly solid, a three-storey mass of brick and stone, stucco and timber that seemed to reach out to her with welcoming arms.

And it would keep her safe. That was how she had always felt about this house, since the day fifteen years ago when her father had first brought her here to visit the Hammonds. So long as she stayed at Safe Harbour, Brodie thought, nothing could ever hurt her.

Jerry stopped his car beside the back door, and Brodie jumped out. She stood on tiptoe to peek into the garage, but the spot where Drew left his Lincoln was empty. She heaved a big sigh, and then had to smile ruefully at her own impatience. Drew would be home soon, and there was plenty of time to tell him about Jerry and the wonderful love they had found in these last few weeks. After all, Drew's law practice was the busiest in town, and she could scarcely expect him to take the afternoon off to wait for her.

Besides, Brodie thought, just now she wanted to throw out her arms and embrace Safe Harbour.

The housekeeper was at the back door. Brodie swept her into a bear hug. 'I'm home!' she carolled.

'I can see,' the woman agreed calmly, but there was a gleam of joy in her eyes. 'And who's this?'

'This is my friend, Jerry Whitcomb. Jerry, this is Mrs

Riley. She's the major-general who keeps us all in line around here.'

'I know you, don't I?' Mrs Riley asked, studying Jerry with narrowed eyes. 'You're one of the Whitcomb kids from down on Cherry Street, aren't you?'

'That's right,' Jerry said. His jaw tightened at the tone of Mrs Riley's voice.

'Jerry's studying business and economics at the University, Mrs Riley,' Brodie put in quickly. 'Since we were both coming back to Hammond's Point, he offered me a ride.'

'I see. Well, bring in your luggage, Brodie. I made those sweet rolls you like so much, if you'd like to ask your friend to stay.' She went back into the kitchen.

'I feel five years old,' Jerry muttered under his breath as he tugged one of Brodie's monogrammed leather bags from the car. 'Do I have to knock on the door and ask if you can come out and play, too?'

'Don't mind Mrs Riley. She thinks I'm still a baby.'

Jerry grunted. 'And since when am I only a friend, Brodie? Was I dreaming last week when you said you'd marry me?'

She gave him a brilliant smile. 'Oh, darling, stop it. I just thought it was only polite to tell Drew first.'

'If I had my way, I'd be announcing it from the treetops without waiting for Mr Wonderful's permission.'

'Why don't you stop worrying about him and come in for one of Mrs Riley's sweet rolls? They absolutely drip butter and nuts and cinnamon.'

'She seems to think I'm a charity case. No, thanks, Brodie. I'll go back to the other side of the tracks where I belong.' His voice held a tinge of bitterness.

'Jerry, really!' Brodie was exasperated. 'At least come for dinner tonight.'

'Must I?'

'You're going to have to meet Drew sometime. It might as well be tonight, so we can get it over with.'

'All right. You win.'

'Seven o'clock. And wear a suit.'

'Too bad my white tie and tails are at the cleaners,' Jerry said sarcastically. He leaned over to kiss her.

Brodie dodged, and said, 'Not here. Too many people can see, and . . .'

'Are you going to turn into a snob on me, Brodie?' The question was sharp. 'Now that you're back home with the country club set——'

'No! But let's wait till we've told Drew, and . . .' Her voice trailed off unhappily.

'All right,' Jerry said gloomily. 'See you at seven.'

He drove off without a backward look, and Brodie stood on the back step for several minutes, lost in thought. She was right, she knew she was. It was only good manners to let Drew announce her engagement, and it would be good politics besides. Drew wouldn't take kindly to the idea of the neighbours knowing about Brodie's young man before he did, and if anything would set his opposition into cement, it would be that.

He wasn't going to like the idea, anyway, she knew. Jerry was right about that much. Drew was a sweetheart, but he was fiercely proud of the Hammond heritage, and for his ward to marry one of the Whitcomb kids . . .

I can talk him around, Brodie thought. There has never been anything I couldn't talk Drew into if I tried hard enough. And I never wanted anything so badly as I want Jerry. When Drew sees how much I love Jerry, he can't say no.

And even if he gets stubborn and refuses his permission, she concluded, September isn't far away, and then I can do as I like.

She took a deep breath of the early summer air, heavily perfumed with the scent of lilacs from the bushes that surrounded the little lattice-work gazebo. All summer, she thought, I'll read, and garden, and lie in the sun. Safe Harbour—could there be anywhere in the world that was more beautiful than Safe Harbour in the summer?

Mrs Riley looked up when Brodie came in, dragging a heavy garment bag. 'Need some help?'

'No. I shipped most of my things. Did I hear you say something about hot rolls?'

Mrs Riley lifted an enormous, puffy pastry out of the pan and slid it on to a plate. Brodie sank on to a stool at the breakfast bar and took a deep breath of the yeasty fragrance. 'I've missed these,' she said: 'Drew is coming home for dinner, isn't he?' It was almost an afterthought.

'He wouldn't dream of missing your first evening at home,' Mrs Riley scolded.

'Good. I invited Jerry, by the way.' Brodie cut into the bread and steam wafted out.

Mrs Riley poured a cup of coffee and set it in front of Brodie. 'The first night you're home? Mr Hammond won't like that.'

'Well, Jerry's kind of special.' She closed her eyes so she could concentrate on the taste of plump raisins, tangy nuts, and sharp cinnamon, and she didn't see the suspicious look that Mrs Riley gave her. 'I would have killed for one of these rolls last week during final exams,' she said.

Mrs Riley didn't answer, and Brodie finished her snack in silence. 'I'm going to take my coffee upstairs and unpack. And I think I'll have a long, hot bubble bath,' she announced.

'They didn't have bathtubs in the dorm?'

'Not like the ones here,' Brodie pointed out with a smile.

The back stairs were closer, but she walked instead down the long walnut-panelled hall and up the wide front staircase with its dark red carpet. Safe Harbour even smells different from other houses, she thought as she reached her own room at the top of the stairs.

It felt wonderful to be home. The big, airy bedroom with its southwest windows was the one she had moved into as a frightened child when her father died. Then it had been bright pink, with ruffles and eyelet lace—someone's mistaken idea of the perfect room for a little girl. Now it was softly feminine in lemon and peach, without a single frill, the perfect background for Brodie's sable-brown hair and dark eyes.

Perhaps we can be married here in the house, she thought as she pinned her hair up off her neck and filled the deep claw-footed tub with frothy bubbles. She would love to walk down the grand staircase on Drew's arm, a long veil trailing over the plush carpet, and across the hall to the big drawing room where Jerry would be waiting . . .

She was thinking about her wedding, with a dreamy smile and her elbows propped on the glass top of her dressing table, when the grandfather clock down in the hall chimed six. It was long past time for Drew to be home, she thought. And then, with growing uneasiness, she wondered if he had come home already and Mrs Riley had told him—what?

Don't be silly, Brodie McKenzie, she told herself firmly as she tugged the skirt of her pale yellow dress into place. In the first place, Mrs Riley didn't know anything worth telling. And Drew would never take Mrs Riley's word as gospel truth; he'd at least ask Brodie first . . . wouldn't he?

Her foot was on the bottom step when he came out of the library, and Brodie seemed to freeze there for a moment.

In other homecomings she would have flung herself into his arms with a squeal of delight, and Drew would have laughed at her excitement and lifted her off her feet for a great warm bear hug. But this time Brodie hovered on the stairs and simply looked at him. Her eyes were nearly on a level with his, with the aid of the stair and her high-heeled sandals.

'So my little lady is growing up,' he said with a smile. 'Are you too old for a hug, Brodie?'

She smiled at the teasing warmth of his voice and came down a step, her hand extended. 'I'll never get too old for that.'

Drew laughed and put a casual arm about her. 'I'm going to have a drink before I change for dinner. Join me?'

She was thinking, as they walked together into the drawing room, about Drew and Safe Harbour. She couldn't imagine him any other place; the big rooms and masculine wood of the house were made for him. To visualise him in a bungalow was ridiculous.

Brodie chose a blue-velvet chair that matched one of the jewel-like colours in the Oriental rug, and watched as he splashed Scotch into a glass and added ice and soda.

He wasn't exactly handsome, she thought as she studied him. But at thirty-three he had the kind of mature, striking attractiveness that makes women of all ages take a second look. For the first time in her life, Brodie felt a twinge of curiosity about the girl who had jilted him so many years ago. She had never heard the whole story. She had been just a child at the time, with only the vaguest recollection of the woman. But she knew that since Cynthia had rejected him, Drew had never been serious about another woman.

What a waste, Brodie thought. No matter who Cynthia was, she couldn't have been worth that.

Drew turned from the trolley and saw the thoughtful look on her face. 'Why so serious?' he asked. 'Mrs Riley tells me we're having a guest for dinner.'

'Do you mind, Drew? I know it's my first night at home, and we always have a quiet evening and catch up on talking, but . . .'

Drew sipped his drink and sat down on the couch. 'I gather that he's a special guest,' he observed.

Brodie sat up straight and twisted her hands together

in her lap. 'A very special guest. My fiancé, in fact.'

Drew's eyebrows shot up. 'Aren't you a little young for this? You have two years of college left.'

'I know what I want, Drew. I want to marry Jerry more than I've ever wanted anything before.'

'Ross Whitcomb's boy.' Drew's voice was dry. 'I don't believe you've had the pleasure of meeting Ross yet.'

'I don't care what Jerry's father has done. I know that he served time in prison—but that has nothing to do with Jerry.'

'That's true,' he admitted.

Brodie pressed her advantage. 'Drew, it isn't like you to form an opinion before you meet him. Jerry is determined to make his own way. He isn't going to stay in that gutter, you'll see.'

'Perhaps I shall.' Drew set his half-full glass back on the cart. 'I'd better go change clothes so I'm prepared to meet this paragon.' He was whistling as he ran up the steps.

Brodie leaned back in her chair with a sigh. The worst hurdle was past; she had broken the news without provoking Drew to an explosion. She frankly wouldn't have been surprised if he had tried to forbid her to see Jerry again. That sort of reaction would have made it a challenge to talk him around.

Perhaps, she thought, Drew would be glad to be rid of her. He'd been responsible for Brodie for more than ten years. It would be no wonder if he was anxious to wash his hands of her.

She was glad that he was being so agreeable. He couldn't have changed her mind, anyway, and it would have been difficult for everyone if he had tried. So why, she asked herself irritably, did she feel disappointed— and more than a little apprehensive?

The conversation at dinner was cool and civil. Drew wasn't making it easy for Jerry, but neither was he using the courtroom cross-examination techniques that had driven more than one of Brodie's past boyfriends out of Safe Harbour in a cold sweat.

And Jerry was doing very well indeed, Brodie thought proudly as she dipped a whole strawberry into the neat pyramid of confectioner's sugar. He looked like the banker he might someday be, in a dark-blue pinstriped suit and discreet tie. He was looking Drew straight in the eyes and answering his questions calmly.

Drew's face, of course, never betrayed his thoughts, but Brodie thought she could see a hint of surprise in his expression.

'I'll be working at Fanning Brother's this summer,' Jerry was saying. 'On the manufacturing line. Though of course I'd love to get my foot in the door at management level.'

Drew nodded. 'That kind of experience would be helpful when you graduate. Unfortunately, positions of that sort are rare.'

'How well I know, sir. But the assembly-line job will help to pay the tuition next year. The Hammonds owned that plant originally, didn't they?'

'Yes. My grandfather sold it to the Fannings, because my father was more interested in law than in producing farm equipment.'

'Safe Harbour,' Jerry mused, and glanced around the dining room at the sparkle of crystal and silver. 'The house that tractors built.' There was a note of irony in his voice.

Brodie knew what he was thinking. Built by the sweat of men who were underpaid and overworked . . . She and Jerry had argued that a dozen times. He was right, as a matter of fact, but that had nothing to do with Drew. She had to step in, to prevent Drew from questioning what Jerry meant.

She looked up at the massive chandelier where hundreds of crystal prisms surrounded a gold pineapple, the symbol of hospitality, and said thoughtfully,

'Actually, it was land speculation to begin with. After that, it was farm equipment, and then . . .'

'Brodie,' Drew said firmly, 'let's not dissect the family fortune tonight, all right? What are you going to do with yourself this summer, my girl?'

'I thought I'd ask the boss for my old job back.'

'What if the position has been filled?' he teased.

'Come on, Drew. You know I'm the best office girl you ever hired.'

'That's probably true,' he mused. 'Very well, Bro, you have a job, whenever you want to start.'

'Next week, all right? I'll take a few days off first. And of course I'll have wedding plans to make,' Brodie added. 'I'll stay busy.'

Drew's forehead wrinkled, and she held her breath for a moment. 'Have you set a date?' he asked finally.

Brodie sent a triumphant look at Jerry. See? it said. I told you he'd let me have whatever I wanted?

'Soon,' Brodie said. 'I can't wait to be Mrs Jerry Whitcomb.'

'I should think it will take a while to get ready,' Drew observed. 'Perhaps the end of August?'

'I don't want to wait that long,' Brodie wailed.

'Oliver Panning won't be pleased if Jerry asks for time off in the middle of the summer for a honeymoon.'

'That's right,' Jerry agreed. 'We'll have to make do with a weekend. In any case I can't afford much of a trip, but . . .'

'Maybe Drew will make that his gift to us,' Brodie suggested, and flashed her most charming smile at him.

It bounced off Drew, who said, 'I'll give it some thought.'

But Brodie wasn't upset. 'Let's go pick out my ring tomorrow, Jerry. Now that it's official . . .'

'It isn't,' Drew said sharply. 'Not till it's been announced.'

'But, Drew!' she protested.

He picked up her hand. 'There will be no ring on this

lovely finger until after the announcement is made.'

Jerry saw the angry colour rise in Brodie's cheeks and intervened. 'We'll do as Drew likes, Brodie.'

'Then at least let's do it right away. Can we have a big party, Drew?' Suddenly Brodie's irritation was gone. 'Invite all my friends—so many of them have never met Jerry. What about Saturday night? Please, Drew? We can be ready by then, I know we can.'

'Very well. Now I'd like to talk to Jerry alone for a while—the proverbial man-to-man chat. So run along, Brodie.'

'I'll be waiting,' she promised blithely. She dropped a kiss on Jerry's cheek and danced out to the kitchen.

'What hit you?' Mrs Riley asked. She was loading plates into the dishwasher.

Brodie almost told her, before she remembered her own warning. It was Drew's job, to announce it. 'We're having a party Saturday night,'she said.

The housekeeper warmed a bit. 'It'll be nice to see Safe Harbour sparkle again.'

'It always sparkles,' Brodie countered.

'Not like it does with a party. It gets kind of lonely with just Mr Hammond here. He eats out a lot, and works all the time. The house just seems kind of bored with it all.'

Brodie was startled. She had never suspected the housekeeper of having an imagination.

'I'll have to start polishing silver tomorrow,' Mrs Riley said, half to herself.

'I'll begin on the guest list right now.' Brodie reached for a notepad and sat down at the breakfast bar. She was still hard at work when Jerry came down the hall.

'I'll see you tomorrow, darling,' he said, bending over her to put a possessive kiss on her lips. 'We'll go pick out your ring, even if you can't wear it just yet.'

Brodie walked out to his car with him, and she was still bubbling when she came back to the kitchen a few minutes later. Mrs Riley was standing in the middle of the kitchen, hands on her hips. 'This is an engagement party?' she asked sharply. 'You're going to marry that young punk?'

'Jerry isn't some kind of delinquent, Mrs Riley,' Brodie began hotly.

Mrs Riley cut her off in midsentence, shaking her head sadly. 'I never thought I'd see such goings-on at Safe Harbour,' she mourned. 'To think that the young lady of this house has so little opinion of herself as to get mixed up with——'

'The young lady of this house knows quite well what she wants, Mrs Riley! And to begin with, I want silence from you—it's none of your business whom I choose to marry!' Brodie stalked out of the room and up the stairs, her temper at white heat.

Drew was in the sitting room next to his bedroom. The room was dim, and the stereo was playing Rachmaninoff. Drew was stretched out in a chair, a magazine on his lap.

'For heaven's sake, Drew, you're going to blind yourself, reading in the dark this way,' Brodie said sharply and snapped a light on.

Drew sat up abruptly, running a hand absently along his jaw as if to reassure himself that he'd shaved.

'I just came in to tell you that Mrs Riley is getting awfully impudent. She seems to think that I'm crazy to marry Jerry.'

'She may have community support.'

'You of all people should understand, Drew. All men are created equal, you know.' Brodie's tone was sarcastic.

'But sometimes they don't stay that way. You've been raised in luxury, Brodie. Just how do you think you and Jerry are going to live for two years till he's self-supporting?'

'We'll manage. I was meaning to ask you about something, Drew.' She curled up in the chair opposite his. 'We've talked before about my college education, and you know that I think it's a waste of time for me. The things I want to do I can't learn in school. I've had all the singing lessons I can absorb. It's time for me to get out and perform and see what I can do.'

'Absolutely not true. Some of the best singers in the world take lessons every day. But something tells me that isn't the bottom line.'

'You're right. I know what these two years of college have cost you, Drew. And I know that you want me to go on.' She took a deep breath. 'So if you're going to spend the money, anyway, why not spend it on someone who's worth it? Instead of paying my tuition next year, will you pay Jerry's?'

'No.' There was not an instant of hesitation.

It took Brodie by surprise. 'But Drew——'

'I'm willing to invest in your future, Brodie. Jerry hasn't shown me anything yet that convinces me to place my bets on him.'

'But Jerry is my future, Drew! His education will mean security for me.'

He shrugged. 'So will yours. And if your marriage breaks up——'

'It won't break up, Drew. I won't let it.'

'Marriage licences don't come with guarantees, Bro. Every divorce I handle is a couple that intended to make it till death us do part.' He looked her over unemotionally. 'Did Jerry ask you to do this?'

'No! He wouldn't ask for anything for himself. He doesn't even know I was thinking about it.' There was a long silence, then she asked hesitantly, 'Will you do it?'

'In words of one syllable, Brodie—no, I won't. I will give you an engagement party and a wedding and a gift of some sort. It will not be the honeymoon, by the way——' He broke off suddenly, shook his head, ran a hand back through his hair to the nape of his neck, as if it was suddenly hurting. 'I have a moral obligation to your father, and mine. But more than that I will not do.

Once married, you aren't my responsibility any more,
Brodie.'

She was stunned. This wasn't the uncle who had
always indulged her whims, the big brother who had
petted and spoiled her. 'I thought—after we were
married——' She stopped and tried again. 'There isn't
any sense in us renting an apartment for a few weeks. I
thought perhaps we could . . .'

'Live here at Safe Harbour?' His smile was twisted.
'No, Brodie. Once you leave this house as Mrs
Whitcomb, you will come back only by invitation.'

Anger swept over her, then. 'You're trying to make
me back down!' she cried. 'You're trying to break us
apart!'

'Not I,' Drew denied. 'I know how foolish that would
be. I'm just presenting the facts, Brodie, so that your
decision is made with full knowledge of the consequences.'

She stormed across the room and turned at the door.
'Well, it isn't going to work, Drew. I'll marry whom I
please, when I please. It's none of your damn business!'

'That's right,' he said calmly. 'You're legally an adult
now. You have every right to make your own mistakes.
But tell me, Brodie, how are you going to eat, next
year?'

'I'll find a job,' she said. 'We can do it. Hamburger
tastes just fine when you eat it with someone you love.'

Drew's eyes went back to his magazine, and
Rachmaninoff blasted forth in a wild Slavic dance.
'How very young you are,' he said. 'How very, very
innocent.' Somehow, in that vibrant voice that could
make a courtroom echo when he chose, it sounded like
a curse.

CHAPTER TWO

DREW was whistling softly through his teeth as he tinkered with the engine of the Lincoln, and the tuneless sound drifting in through the kitchen window was like sandpaper on Brodie's nerves as she polished a silver tray.

He'd parked the car just outside the back door when he'd come home from playing golf at the country club, and he had been head-first into the motor for almost two hours. Brodie suspected darkly that there was nothing wrong with the car; Drew just didn't want to come into Safe Harbour today because somebody might hand him a polishing cloth. Brodie sighed heavily and put the gleaming tray aside.

Across the table sat her best friend from college, her face reflecting Brodie's frustration. 'We've been polishing silver for hours,' Janet said finally. 'How many candlesticks does it take to light this house?'

'You'd be amazed,' Brodie said.

Mrs Riley looked up from the sink where she was slicing raw vegetables for the dips. 'There's iced tea in the refrigerator,' she said. 'Have a break, girls. Take Mr Hammond a glass, Brodie.'

Brodie looked sullen, but she took three glasses down from the cabinet. It was no use arguing with Mrs Riley; the ice still hadn't cracked since their quarrel, though it had been almost a week.

She paused and admired the cake that stood on the tea trolley in the corner of the kitchen, ready to be rolled into the drawing room tonight as soon as the announcement was made. 'Best Wishes, Brodie and Jerry,' it said in icing, with a pair of hands holding wedding rings in the centre. Brodie smiled to herself.

Tonight it would all be official. Tonight she could put on the lovely diamond ring they had chosen so carefully . . .

Janet held the back door open. 'Let's go sit in the gazebo,' she said.

It was warm in the afternoon sun, not a cloud in the sky, the flower-scented breeze whispering across the hill. Drew had taken his shirt off and draped it over the Lincoln's bonnet. 'Here's a glass of tea, Drew,' Brodie said politely, wishing that she dared to just pour it, ice cubes and all, down his bare back.

That quarrel hadn't eased yet, either. She was coolly polite to Drew, whenever she couldn't avoid him. He didn't seem to notice.

'Thanks.' He turned abruptly, and his oily hand brushed hers as he took the glass.

Brodie didn't answer. She crossed the drive to the little white gazebo where Janet had already stretched out.

'I don't believe how good-looking he is.' Janet sipped her tea. 'I've never known a man with green eyes before. And just look at those muscles.'

'Do you mean Drew?'

'Do you see any other green-eyed, shirtless males around? Of course I mean Drew. Do you expect me to believe that you've never noticed?'

Brodie shrugged and let her fingers trail through the cool water of the fountain, rubbing them together to remove the oil. 'Why should I notice? He's only my guardian.'

'With Drew as an example, I can't imagine you falling for Jerry Whitcomb.'

'I thought you liked Jerry.'

'I do, but he's really not marriageable material, Bro.'

'And you think Drew is? Let me fill you in.'

Janet sat up straight. 'I thought you never would. Come on, Brodie. All the details.'

'His heart was broken years ago and has never

healed.' Brodie threw her arms out in a melodramatic gesture. 'And ever since the fair Cynthia told him to darken her door no more . . .'

'Your poetry is dreadful.'

'He has mourned for her in the secret recesses of his heart, and . . .'

'That's mourning? To me, he looks like a healthy male animal enjoying himself.'

'He conceals it well.'

'Sure.' Janet took her gaze off Drew for a minute to eye Brodie speculatively. 'Does he like blondes? Should I come on soft and clinging, or assertive?'

'How should I know? No woman has got close to him in ten years.'

'Some friend you are.' Janet sank back on the bench. 'Though I'm awfully glad you invited me to your party.'

'Even if you have to help polish silver?'

'To be scrupulously honest, I did volunteer,' Janet admitted. 'Why does Mrs Riley use your first name, and call him Mr Hammond?'

'Because he is the master of the house and I am only the poor waif that the family took in to keep from starving.'

'I've seen your wardrobe in the past year, and I can say without hesitation that I'd like to be one of Drew Hammond's charities. Where do I apply?'

'There will be an opening as soon as I'm married, that's sure.'

It was no surprise to Janet; they'd talked till the wee hours of the morning, sprawled across Brodie's bed, catching up on the details of the past week. 'Can he really do that?' Janet asked. 'Cut you off without a dime, I mean.'

'Oh, yes, he can do it. Drew isn't obliged to support me all my life. And I didn't ask him to,' she said with sudden bitterness. 'All I asked for was a helping hand to get us started.'

'Maybe he has his reasons, Brodie.'

'Oh, come on, Jan. Don't you start defending him! I invited you to Safe Harbour this weekend because you're my closest friend and the only one who doesn't preach to me about what I owe Drew. Well, I don't owe him anything.'

'Are you certain?' Brodie made a threatening gesture, and Janet said hastily, 'All right, I'll quit.' There was a long silence. 'What are you going to do, Bro?'

'As soon as we go back to school, I'll start looking for a job. There are nightclubs all over that town. I'll be what I've always wanted to be—a singer.'

Janet shook her head. 'Most of those so-called nightclubs are only bars, Bro. And you can't make a living doing that.'

'I've had years and years of singing lessons.'

'I know, and you have a lovely voice. But it's a college town. There are people willing to perform for nothing, just to get the experience. Who's going to pay you?'

'Then I'll get another sort of job.'

'Why don't you be sensible? Postpone your wedding and stay in school. Starving in a garret for the sake of love may sound romantic to you, but it just makes it harder on Jerry. If you wait till he graduates——'

Brodie's chin set stubbornly. 'We'll make it together,' She swirled the ice cubes in her glass. 'And maybe Drew won't carry out his threat after all. He seems to be getting used to Jerry. He even invited him to play golf today.' But her voice lacked conviction.

Safe Harvour was glowing by the time they were done. The buffet table was set up in the dining room with fresh flowers from the garden scenting the air, crystal glasses shining and the finest of fragile china ready to use. The drawing room floor, under the Oriental rug, was polished to a gleam, and the doors to the terrace stood open to the warm breeze.

How lucky Drew was that all of this was his, Brodie

thought as she walked through on a final inspection. A flicker of jealousy ran along her spine.

The house seemed happy, expectant—almost as if it were humming a tune. That's a silly thought, Brodie, she told herself. It's only the plumbing and the refrigerator that you're hearing. But Safe Harbour did seem to her to have a personality all its own. It wanted to be busy, and warm, and well-lighted. It needed an active family—kids to run through the halls and slide down the bannisters. She started to laugh at the very idea. Drew, the perennial bachelor, with a houseful of kids? 'At least he could get a dog,' Brodie muttered under her breath and went to the kitchen to have a quick snack before she changed clothes.

Drew was still working on the Lincoln. He'd apparently finished with the motor, though, and was now buffing the dark grey finish to a shine. He'd always taken good care of his cars, Brodie thought idly, but never before had she known him to spend an entire afternoon manicuring one.

He was still shirtless, and he was sweating under the warm sun as he rubbed the chamois over the bonnet. Brodie wondered if Janet would find him as attractive now. Probably she would. She might even be hanging out the window of the guest room, above the drive, to get the best possible view.

Just what was it that Janet saw in Drew, Brodie wondered. He was good-looking, but he was more than a dozen years older than Janet. From Brodie's perspective, thirty-three seemed ancient. Oh, well, she decided, if Janet wanted to waste her time flirting with Drew, it was none of Brodie's business.

She fixed herself a ham and cheese sandwich and wandered outside, thinking vaguely that she should try to talk to Drew. The last few days had been unpleasantly silent. She didn't want her engagement party spoiled by this cloud that was hanging over them.

'Why aren't you using the electric buffer I got you last Christmas?' she asked.

Drew looked up and brushed sweat off his forehead with the back of his hand. 'Sometimes it's more satisfying to do it by hand.'

Brodie didn't understand that at all, but she didn't press it. 'Shouldn't you quit soon? The party starts in a couple of hours.'

'I'll be ready. Nobody will care what I look like, anyway—all eyes will be on you.'

She pulled up a lawn chair and sat down. 'Do you think anybody suspects what the party is all about?'

He laughed. 'In Hammond's Point? If you wanted to keep it a secret, you and Romeo should have gone farther than Brooke's Jewellery to buy your ring, Brodie.'

'I wish you wouldn't call Jerry that, Drew.'

'Why not? It seems to me there are a lot of similarities.' He stepped back to inspect his work, then started to rub out a smudge on the driver's door.

'I know you don't think he's a good choice, but the fact is, he's the man I love, Drew.'

'At twenty, my dear, girls don't know what the hell love is all about. They think it's some kind of game.'

'I'm not like Cynthia, Drew!' The words burst out, and then Brodie bit her tongue. Never had she dared to say that name to him; as far as she knew, no one had mentioned his lost love to him in years. She swallowed hard, wondering if she had poured salt in his old wounds.

Drew laughed sharply. 'Cynthia was an expert at the game, that's sure,' he said. 'Obviously we aren't going to agree on this—and I don't want to quarrel with you, Bro. Let's call a truce, all right?'

'I don't want to argue either,' Brodie said softly. She was rewarded with a brilliant smile before he bent his head to his work again.

'Drew——' she said hesitantly, a little later. 'Jerry

and I were talking about the wedding. We'd like you to
sing—would you? You have such a beautiful voice, and
it would mean so much to me.'

His hand slipped on the polishing cloth and the heavy
ring on his right hands squealed across the satin finish
of the Lincoln's paint. 'Damn!' he said, and bent over
to inspect the long scratch. 'Hand me that can of wax,
Brodie.'

Brodie watched in silence as he poured out a pool of
liquid and rubbed it into the bonnet in ever-widening
circles. Finally, she said, 'Will you, Drew?'

'Will I what? Oh, you mean sing.' He was absorbed
in making the scratch disappear. 'I think I'll have plenty
to do just by giving you away, Bro. I wouldn't want to
steal the show.' He looked up then, with a smile that
didn't quite reach his eyes. 'If you're finished with your
sandwich, how about making me one?'

'Sure.' She picked up her plate and started for the
house. It was silly to be unhappy about it; she hadn't
really expected that Drew would agree. Brodie had
discovered her own love of music in the duets they
used to sing, but he seldom used that gorgeous
baritone in public. He might agree eventually, she
thought, if she could just convince him how important
it was to her.

She was spreading mustard on his ham and cheese,
careful to get it just the way he liked it, when Jerry
knocked at the back door. 'You're early,' she said,
raising her face for his kiss. Then she noticed his jeans
and plimsolls.

'I need to talk to you, Brodie. Then I'll go home and
get dressed.'

'It'll have to be fast. I still have to take a shower, and
I haven't done a thing to my hair.' She brushed a
careless hand over the sable ponytail. 'Even Jan is
already getting dressed.'

'It won't take long.' Jerry looked worried. 'Brodie,
maybe we shouldn't go ahead with the party tonight.'

She stared up at him. 'What do you mean? Not announce our engagement?'

He nodded. 'You didn't tell me what Hammond said to you about us getting married. But you've let little things drop here and there, and I suspect—the more I think about it—that it was plenty nasty. So it's time for the truth.'

'He's coming around. And anyway, I didn't want to upset you, Jerry.'

'Don't you think I ought to know? Brodie, what did he tell you? All of it.'

She ducked her head and repeated, slowly and expressionlessly, all she could remember of her conversation with Drew.

When she had finished, Jerry was silent. 'I don't believe that you didn't tell me this before, Brodie. The man as good as told you he was finished with you as soon as we get married.'

'What difference does it make? He's only my guardian for another four months, Jerry. Then he'd be through with me anyway.'

'But in the meantime he isn't going to let you have a cent. We can't live till September without any money, Bro. Be reasonable!'

'Jerry, we both have jobs. We——'

'You'll be getting pin money playing messenger girl at his law firm,' he said curtly. 'How long do you think that will last once we're married?'

It was unanswerable. Brodie hadn't even considered that Drew might not want her working in his office, either.

'And I'm not saving much from my salary,' Jerry added, 'even by living at home where it's free. If I add the expense of rent and groceries—there just won't be enough money.'

'We'll make it, Jerry. We'll be careful.'

His voice was cold. 'Obviously you have never lived on a budget.'

'I can learn.' Brodie's tone bristled with irritation. 'Nobody thinks I can do anything.'

'Well, getting married this summer is out. We'll just wait till September.'

'What's magical about September?'

'You'll be twenty-one. Unless——' He shook his head. 'There has to be a way to shake some cash out of him to help us out.'

'There isn't, Jerry. It's his money, and if he doesn't want . . .'

'But dammit, Brodie, you have a right . . .' Then, abruptly, he stopped. 'What did you say?'

'I said, Drew can spend his money however he wants. He isn't obligated to give any of it to me. What's the matter with you, Jerry? You're the financial expert.'

He shook his head as if to clear it. 'What about your money?'

'What money?'

He spoke slowly, as if explaining to a kindergartener. 'The money you will get control of on your next birthday. Unless Hammond finds a way to mess that up, too.'

Brodie started to laugh. 'The McKenzies never managed to accumulate enough cash to need a bank account, Jerry. If you want to talk about coming from the wrong side of the tracks, I'm right there with you. The only thing of value that my father possessed was a good friend named Andy Hammond.' But her mirth died quickly when there was no answering laughter from Jerry. 'It doesn't matter, does it, Jerry?' Her voice was hollow. 'Does it?'

He dropped into a chair at the breakfast bar, and she read his reply in the stricken eyes he raised to her.

'What did you think, Jerry?' she asked through dry lips.

'The same thing everyone else did,' he said quietly, 'from the time we were kids in kindergarten. You might

as well have been a Hammond, the way you dressed—
the way you lived.'

'I could scarcely live any other way at Safe Harbour,
Jerry,' she pointed out, 'Andy treated me as his
daughter.'

He sighed heavily. 'That does it. It was true, after all.'

'What was true?' But there was no answer. 'It's all
right, Jerry,' she said softly, 'if you don't think we can
manage the finances now, then we'll just wait a couple
of years, till you're through school. It's no big deal. We
have plenty of time.'

'You might have time,' he said bitterly. 'And so do
I—only mine is called time payments. Brodie, be
sensible. How do you think a guy like me managed to
buy that diamond ring of yours?'

'I thought—you said you'd saved some money . . .'

His laugh was a sneer. 'Enough to buy that rock?
Not quite. After all, you can't give a diamond chip to a
girl who lives in a house like this, Brodie.'

'I'd rather have a chip that's mine than a full carat
that isn't paid for.' Her voice broke.

'Well, I couldn't even have afforded the chip,' Jerry
said tartly. 'I borrowed five hundred bucks from a guy
at work for the down-payment—told him I'd pay him
back as soon as we were married.'

Her dark eyes were filled with horror. 'You expected
that Drew would pay for my engagement ring?'

'No. But I thought once we were married and you
were getting a bigger allowance . . .' He slammed his fist
down on the countertop. 'Oh, hell.'

'We'll have to take the ring back. It's not the end of
the world, Jerry. I'd like to have a diamond, but——'
she tried to laugh off her disappointment as she looked
down at the bare finger that would never wear that
lovely ring. 'Maybe someday we can afford it.'

He looked up at her, astounded. 'You really don't
understand, do you, Brodie? It isn't just whether we buy
a rock or not. There's tuition next fall, and living

expenses, and the debts I've already run up. I can't meet the bills without some help.'

'We can borrow the money——'

'Banks frown on loaning money to students who aren't making passing grades.' He laughed, then. 'Surprised, Brodie? I don't know why you should be. Last semester I was working two jobs, plus romancing you. What a waste of time.'

She flinched away from his cruel words.

'I grew up pinching pennies and hoping that my luck would change—living in that rundown house with eight other people. I don't want to wait for "someday" to come along. I want the good things now! Don't you see, Brodie?'

She was silent, listening to her dream world cave in under her feet. 'When you thought I was rich, Jerry, it was convenient to be in love with me. Now that I'm just another girl——'

'Dammit, Brodie, you lied to me!' His chair went spinning across the floor as he crossed the room in a lunge. His face was red and his eyes blazed.

Brodie shrank from the sharpness in his voice. 'I didn't lie, Jerry.' He's going to strike me, she thought, and raw fear choked her throat. Jerry—the man I love—is going to hit me.

The back door banged as Drew burst into the room. 'Whitcomb,' he warned, his voice like a lash. 'If you so much as touch her, you'll spend the night in jail.'

For a second, Brodie thought Jerry hadn't heard. But then reason dawned in his eyes, and his hands dropped.

Drew didn't take his eyes off Jerry. 'Go to your room, Bro,' he ordered.

She slid past Jerry and paused in the doorway. 'Thanks, Drew.' She managed to choke the words out. Then, her whole body trembling, she climbed the back stairs. She felt eighty years old.

She stood just inside the door of her room for a moment, and then flung herself across the bed, heedless of the ivory dress so carefully laid out for her party.

'My engagement party,' she said, her voice breaking, and pushed the dress into a heap at the end of the bed with a contemptuous hand. She closed her eyes and willed the tears to come, but his heartbreak was too deep to cry away. She lay dry-eyed and tense till the tap sounded on her door.

'Brodie?'

She ignored him, and a couple of minutes later Drew pushed the door open.

'Are you all right, Bro?'

'Is he gone?'

Drew sat down on the edge of her bed, his hand gentle on her shoulder. 'He won't be back, Brodie.'

'I was so scared, Drew.' She twisted around on the satin coverlet and huddled into his arms. It was a haven she had often used. He'd put his shirt back on, and she let her head rest on the smooth fabric, damp with his sweat. It was some comfort to be close to him. Nothing could happen to her as long as she was here at Safe Harbour . . . But it had.

'You don't need to be afraid now.' Drew let his cheek rest against her soft hair and continued to talk, soothing nothings murmured into her ear, until the trembling stopped and she lay passive in his arms.

Brodie sniffed then and said hesitantly, 'Did he tell you what happened?'

'I heard most of it. The window was open, you know. I didn't intend to interfere, but when he came after you like that . . .'

Brodie shivered and hid her face against his shoulder.

'Sorry. I shouldn't have reminded you.' His fingertips brushed gently down her cheek. 'It's time for you to be in the shower. You can't be late to your own party, Bro.'

She jerked out of his arms. 'I'd forgotten about the party.'

Drew glanced at the clock on her dressing table. 'You have half an hour to make yourself presentable.'

'I'm not coming down, Drew. I can't.'

'Yes, you can. And you have to. If you hide up here, everybody in town will know you're nursing a broken heart before the evening is out. Do you want that?'

'No,' she said uncertainly, 'but . . .'

He stood up, retrieved her dress from the carpet where it had slid into a heap, and draped it over a chair. 'You're the one who broke the engagement, remember?'

'It didn't feel that way to me,' Brodie grumbled.

'It has to look like it was your idea, Bro.'

'Why? Because Hammonds don't get jilted?' Abruptly, she realised that for the second time in a single day, she'd thrown Cynthia in his face. She saw that his green eyes had hardened, and she looked away and stumbled on. 'Well, I'm not a Hammond, Drew. I'm no better than Jerry is, and . . .'

Anger crackled in his voice. 'Don't you ever say that again, Brodie McKenzie. Jerry is a fortune-hunting con artist who would run over his grandmother if she happened to get in his way. You're——' he stopped suddenly, and then went on quietly. 'You're sweet and honest and true. Don't put yourself down on his level. Now come on, and get dressed.'

'I can't face all those people.' Her voice was muffled by her pillow.

'You have to face them sometime. Would you rather wait till next week, when all the gossips will be happily searching for signs of a broken heart?'

'I can't do it, Drew.'

'Yes, you can. You have my support, and Janet's. Even Mrs Riley is on your side—when I came upstairs she was singing as she put that fancy cake down the garbage disposal one slice at a time.'

'She never did like Jerry.'

'At the risk of saying I told you so—perhaps her instincts were better than yours. Get up, Brodie.'

'No.'

There was a brief silence. Then Drew spoke from the doorway, and there was no cajoling humour left in his voice. 'Brodie, I'm only going to say this once more. You will get dressed and come down to that party and put a good face on this situation, one way or the other.'

'To save your face, you mean,' Brodie said bitterly.

He didn't answer. 'I'm going to take a shower. If you aren't ready by the time I come back to check on you, I will take you downstairs as you are—but you will appear at this party. Understood?'

He took her rebellious silence for assent, and let the door click shut behind him. And Brodie, because she knew from long experience that even she couldn't push Drew past a certain point, forced herself to sit up on the edge of the bed. He wouldn't back down, and though her nerves were as raw as if they'd been scraped, he would not let her avoid this ordeal.

'Why won't he just let me crawl into the dark somewhere?' she asked plaintively. But the silent room didn't answer.

CHAPTER THREE

MUTED laughter and the sound of glasses clinking floated up the staircase, and Brodie took a deep, steadying breath. 'I can't do it, Jan,' she said.

Janet squeezed her hand reassuringly. 'The longer you put it off, the harder it will be,' she said. 'Besides, Bro, they're your friends.'

'They're just as friendly as a school of sharks,' Brodie mused. 'Once they scent blood——' That was exactly what Drew had meant, she realised. And it was her blood that he was trying to save. She took a reluctant step forward.

The drawing room was full of people, and the crowd had spilled out on to the terrace. For one terrifying moment, Brodie thought she was going to faint. Then she fixed a plastic smile on her lips and moved forward into the crowd.

No one seemed to notice. That was the amazing thing. Janet's skillful use of make-up had disguised Brodie's shock-white face, and the horror in her eyes had dimmed. She moved through the crowd, listening to the compliments from people she hadn't seen in months, introducing Janet, overhearing bits of conversation. She felt as if she wasn't really there. None of this was happening, she was thinking, and the awful scene in the kitchen an hour ago had been just a nightmare. Surely soon she would wake up.

'Would you get me another glass of champagne, Drew?' she asked him quietly, midway through the party.

'I'd rather you stayed with fruit juice tonight.'

Her temper flared instantly. 'It's none of your business what I drink!' she snapped.

'If you want to get drunk after the party, I'll even mix the martinis, Bro. But you don't need a pain-killer right now.'

'You always think you know best, don't you?' she said bitterly, and moved away to get her own champagne.

She saw, out of the corner of her eye, that one of their neighbours had nudged Drew. 'Brodie has become a remarkably pretty woman, Drew,' he said, with a knowing smile. 'Better watch out, or someone's going to snatch her right out from under your nose.'

Drew sipped his champagne. 'Brodie knows that she has a home at Safe Harbour as long as she wants to stay here.'

'Come now. That wasn't what I meant, Drew, and you know it. Better marry her yourself, and keep it all in the family.'

She couldn't hear Drew's reply as she walked away, but the man's assumption made her angry. Did everyone in Hammond's Point think that her father had left her a fortune? she wondered angrily. She had always assumed that everyone knew the truth—that John McKenzie had pawned his last possession to get them home to Hammond's Point when the end was near. For all she knew, Brodie reflected, Andy Hammond might even have paid for that last long bus ride . . .

But at least, she thought, it was some comfort to know that Drew wasn't going to hold a grudge.

Suddenly aware that she was being watched, she turned from the buffet table to meet big blue eyes. The girl who was watching her hardly looked old enough to be included in the party; she was a tiny thing with fluffy blonde hair. She can't be more than eighteen, Brodie thought, and she looked even more ill-at-ease than Brodie felt.

Touched by the girl's plight, she strolled across to take the chair next to the blonde's. 'I don't think I know you,' she said gently. 'And I thought I'd met everyone in Hammond's Point. You can't let my record be spoiled, you know.'

The girl laughed nervously. 'I'm Isabel Fanning. And I've just come back from school in Switzerland, so that's why you don't remember me. I knew you right away, though.'

And why on earth don't Swiss boarding schools teach girls how to get along at social functions? Brodie wondered. Or perhaps they did. She vaguely remembered Isabel now from childhood—a shy, self-effacing little thing, a couple of years younger than Brodie, that no one ever noticed. Perhaps the boarding school had done as much as it could for Isabel Fanning.

'Are you home for the summer, then?'

Isabel gulped her punch nervously. 'I graduated, you see, and I think Daddy's going to let me go to college here. If I go to college at all, that is. I'm not sure I'm smart enough. And I don't want to go back to Europe. I'm not very good at languages, and . . .' She chattered on for a few minutes, and then stopped abruptly, her face red. 'I'm so sorry. I must be boring you to death. Daddy always tells me I don't know when to stop blithering away.'

And no doubt Daddy was the source of most of Isabel's insecurity, Brodie thought. 'Do you know, I've never been to Europe. I guess all I ever wanted to see was Safe Harbour.'

'Oh, it's lovely, isn't it?' Isabel looked around at the gleaming dining room with the delicate tracery in the plaster ceiling, the deep plush carpeting, the bay window. 'You're so lucky to live here. I wish our house looked as nice. Daddy spent all kinds of money on it, but it doesn't look right, somehow. It's knowing how to do it, I think. And I don't know what to do to make it pretty. Do you think you—Oh, there I go again.' She had blushed bright red. 'I've only just met you, and here I am asking for favours.' Her voice had faded off to an embarrassed little whimper, and she looked as if she'd like to hide under her chair.

'Please, Isabel. I'd like to help you, if I can. I'm not a decorator, but . . .' You would also like to bring home every stray dog you see, Brodie told herself firmly. Here you are with a pet—and if you aren't careful, you'll end up with a slave for life. Had no one ever been kind to the child?

'Is Isabel bothering you, Miss McKenzie?' a voice boomed beside her, and Isabel seemed to shrink in her chair.

'Of course not, Mr Fanning,' Brodie said firmly. 'She was just asking about my college, and I've invited her to tea one day next week so we can talk about it.'

'Thank you,' Isabel muttered when her father had moved on. And then, hesitantly, 'Did you really mean it, about coming to tea?'

'Of course. Is Tuesday all right? We don't have to talk about college, either, if you don't choose.' She stood up with a smile. 'But you mustn't let me monopolise you now. I'll expect you Tuesday.'

Isabel gave her an adoring smile, and Brodie's heart warmed. The child had a certain charm, and if someone would just take some time with her . . .

'Hello, Brodie!' The woman who greeted her as she re-entered the drawing room was large and sharp-eyed. 'Where's your young man tonight? Or isn't there going to be an announcement after all?'

It seemed to Brodie that a hush dropped over the room, and she realised abruptly that she'd become so intrigued by Isabel Fanning that—for those few minutes—she had actually stopped thinking about Jerry.

She smiled at the woman. 'An announcement, Mrs Percy?' she asked gently.

'Yes, dear. It was your young man I saw you with in Brooke's this week, wasn't it? You were looking at engagement rings.'

The hush wasn't in Brodie's imagination now. Across

the room she saw Janet pause in mid-motion. A little
closer, Drew's dark green eyes met and held hers,
sending a wave of strength across the crowd. Now's the
time for the performance of your life, Bro, he seemed to
be saying. Caroline Percy was the worst gossip in
Hammond's Point, and if Brodie couldn't convince
her——

Brodie's forehead wrinkled and she looked thoughtful. 'My young man?' she questioned. 'Oh! You must
mean Jerry Whitcomb.' Her puzzlement eased, she
smiled at her tormentor. 'You actually thought that
Jerry and I . . . Now, really, Mrs Percy.' Her smile was
gentle.

Caroline Percy started to stammer, but Brodie cut
through the confusion. 'Jerry was buying a gift for his
mother, and he needed a feminine point of view—you
know how hopeless men are when it comes to knowing
what a woman would like.'

'All men?' Drew asked casually, at her elbow.

Brodie gave him a blinding smile. 'Don't be
conceited about your good taste in jewellery, Drew.'
Her fingertips caressed the gold chain at her throat;
he'd given it to her last Christmas. 'I hate to admit it
with the jeweller in the next room, but looking at
engagement rings was something of a game.' Her
mind was whirling, and she felt as if she were
babbling. She looked up at Drew for encouragement.
His strength steadied her, and she turned back to her
questioner with a smile. 'Mrs Percy, you surely can't
blame me for pretending, just for a bit, that the ring
was mine. It was beautiful.' Her voice caught on the
last word, and she swallowed hard.

Drew stepped in to change the subject, and Brodie
escaped to the terrace, and then on to the formal
garden. She wandered along the flagstone paths, letting
the evening air cool her flushed cheeks.

'The worst is over, Brodie,' she told herself. 'The
worst is over.'

But the pain didn't ease. Janet stayed an extra day, and it was almost a relief for Brodie to see her go. Janet was too much a part of the happy days with Jerry, when love was light-hearted and life was almost too beautiful to bear. On Monday afternoon, she waved goodbye to Janet from the end of the driveway, and then wandered back up to the house.

Safe Harbour was quiet again, as if it were slumbering in the summer sun. The excitement was over; the house would wait patiently, cat-like for the next event. Brodie sat down at the grand piano in the drawing room and played a scale. She should practise, she knew. It had been days since she had even warmed up, and if she wasn't careful, she would lose the professional polish that hundreds of expensive lessons had put on her voice. But she was too lazy today, so she walked down the long cool hall instead and pulled up a stool in the kitchen.

Late afternoon sun was slanting in the windows, making bright pools on the kitchen carpet. Soon Drew would be home. They would have dinner and Mrs Riley would leave and then another endless evening would stretch out in front of her.

At least tomorrow she could go down to the law office, Brodie thought with a sigh. It would help to occupy a few hours in a summer that suddenly seemed to stretch out forever. And Isabel would be coming to tea . . .

Mrs Riley was tearing lettuce for a salad. She looked up with a sympathetic gleam in her eyes when Brodie came in, but she didn't say anything. Brodie was glad; it wouldn't have taken much to bring her to tears.

'Is that Beef Wellington I smell?' Brodie asked. 'It sounds a little heavy for a summer evening.'

Mrs Riley sighed. 'It's Mr Baxter's favourite.'

'Did Drew invite him for dinner?' She didn't sound interested. Daniel Baxter was Drew's partner in the law firm, and he'd never been one of Brodie's favourite people.

Mrs Riley put down her knife, surprise and concern warring in her face. 'Brodie, I heard Mr Hammond tell you last night that he'd invited Mr Baxter.'

'Perhaps he did,' Brodie agreed without interest. 'I mustn't have been listening.'

She heard the Lincoln as it turned into the driveway, and by the time Drew got out of the car she was waiting beside the garage door.

'This is flattering,' he said, with a raised eyebrow. 'Are you eager to share my charming company, or is there something else on your mind?'

'I missed you today. Janet went home a while ago, and it's lonely here.'

He smiled down at her. 'Mrs Riley is here, Bro.' But she knew, deep in her heart, that he understood. He reached into the car for his jacket and his attaché case.

'You aren't going to work tonight, are you?' she asked sadly.

'If the mood strikes.' He stopped in the kitchen for a tall glass of iced tea. Brodie trailed through the house behind him, feeling something like a forlorn puppy. Drew put the attaché case on his desk and sat down in the big leather chair. 'Why didn't you invite Janet to stay?'

'She has a job. Besides——' Brodie shrugged and didn't bother to finish.

'You could ask her to come back next weekend.'

Brodie perched on the arm of his chair. 'Did you like her, Drew?' Was she imagining things? It sounded to her as if Janet had made more of an impression on Drew than Brodie had thought possible.

He shrugged. 'She's a nice kid.'

Brodie let it drop. If Drew really wanted to see Janet, he'd mention her again. And perhaps in a couple of weeks Brodie would be eager for the company. Just now she thought that if she had to entertain anyone ever again, she'd go off in a corner and quietly fall to pieces.

Drew pulled his tie loose with a sigh.

'Tough day?' Brodie asked sympathetically.

'More than the usual share of crazies,' he agreed. 'And my secretary stayed home with a summer cold.' He put a hand to the back of his neck.

'Here. Let me massage it.' Brodie pulled his hand away and started to rub the tense muscles, her thumbs digging gently at the base of his neck. 'I'll come in tomorrow.'

'Sue should be back. But you'd be useful in any case. Would you like to go down to the lake in the afternoon? Take the boat out—maybe do a little fishing?'

'That sounds wonderful!' Brodie threw her arms around him, almost upsetting them both. 'But can you just leave the office like that?'

'I haven't had an afternoon off in weeks.'

'I'll ask Mrs Riley to pack a picnic. Oh—I forgot, Drew. I can't go tomorrow.' Her eyes were sad.

'What's the matter, brat?'

'I invited Isabel Fanning to tea. She'd be crushed if I cancelled.'

'Oliver stopped in today and said you'd befriended his girl.' Drew's tone was casual. 'It's all right, Bro. We'll go to the lake another time.'

She started to rub his back again. 'I didn't think much of Oliver Fanning, that's sure. He's so overwhelming that Isabel is afraid of him. She apparently has never made a decision for herself, poor girl.'

'I don't think I had ever met her before that party,' Drew said thoughtfully.

'Even if you had, you wouldn't remember. She's like a little white mouse huddled in a corner.' She ran her knuckles down his spine and started again at the top of his neck, working her long fingers through his soft dark hair.

He caught her hand and pulled it away from his head. 'Brodie—that's enough.'

She was startled. 'You used to like to have me give you a back rub, Drew. What's the matter?'

She hadn't seen him at a loss for words in a long time. Finally he said, 'Not today, Bro.' He smiled, but it didn't quite reach his eyes. 'Your fingers are very strong. It must be all that piano practise. Have you ever considered being a physical therapist?'

Brodie thought it was a poor effort at humour. 'No, Drew. You know quite well I'm going to be a singer.' She slid off the arm of his chair and started for the door, then paused to toy with the chess set, a game half-played, that stood on a little inlaid table near the door. 'Looks like black is in trouble,' she observed.

'That's the spot Daniel left me in two weeks ago. It's taken this long for me to find a way out, but I think I can finish him off tonight.' Drew snapped the attaché case open and pulled out a stack of files.

'By the way, Drew . . .'

He looked up, eyes narrowed. 'Out with it, Bro,' he ordered. 'I learned long ago to be wary whenever you said "by the way, Drew" in that sweet little voice.'

She picked up the ivory king. 'I don't think I'll go back to school this fall.'

There was a brief silence. 'You haven't already dropped out, have you?'

'No. I'm just not going back. I've never been very happy there, so it's not a sudden decision.'

'Nevertheless, it's being made under stress. Wait a while, Brodie. You may change your mind, once you have a chance to get over Jerry.'

'I don't want to go back,' she said firmly. She stopped at the door and leaned her cheek against the back of her hand, poised on the fine-grained woodwork. 'And as for getting over Jerry,' she said quietly. 'Tell me, Drew—does one ever forget the first love?'

He was silent for a long time, and then he looked up. His face was frozen, and for a moment, when she saw the pain in his eyes, she regretted reminding him of Cynthia.

'No, Brodie,' he said softly. 'You never forget your first love.' And then, as if to himself, he added, 'You love her till you die.'

Daniel Baxter was a bluff, hearty, outgoing man. Perhaps that was why she'd never liked him, Brodie thought during dinner. She'd never believed that he was real. He'd been Andy's partner for years, before Drew went into the firm at all, and Brodie's first memories of Daniel were the vague ones of childhood. He would put her on his knee and playfully pull her curls and tell Andy how pretty she was, and even at the age of five Brodie hadn't trusted him. Fifteen years later, she still didn't. She had no doubt of his legal expertise; Drew would never put up with mediocrity in a partner. But she just didn't like the man.

'Too bad I had to miss your welcome-home party, Brodie,' he said, over the blueberry cheesecake. 'Though I had heard there was a little more than a welcome in the wind.'

'You can hear almost anything from the gossips in this town, Daniel.' Drew didn't sound interested. 'The sooner you learn to ignore half of it, the easier it will be on your ears.'

'You never have let gossip bother you, have you, Drew?' his partner asked curiously. 'With the things that have been said about you over the years . . .'

What things, Brodie wondered. Drew was the most honest, upright and straightforward person she'd ever known. What evidence could the gossips have against him? But of course, that sort of person—people like Caroline Percy—never bothered with evidence.

'Perhaps I've just never let it show, Daniel. You'd better watch yourself at chess tonight, by the way. I have your downfall plotted.'

Daniel laughed, and just then Mrs Riley came to the dining room door. 'There's a telephone call for you, Mr Hammond. It's the one you've been waiting for.'

Drew tossed his napkin down. 'If you'll excuse me?' he said. 'This is an important matter. Please go ahead with coffee.'

'The boy works too hard,' Daniel complained, and held out his cup.

Brodie refilled it from the heavy silver pot at her elbow. 'His practice is the most important thing in his life.'

'I know. And just why is it, that's what I'd like to find out. The boy's young, he needs some recreation.' He leered at her, just a little. 'If you know what I mean.'

Brodie bit her lip. 'He isn't a boy, Daniel, he's a man,' she pointed out as gently as she could. She must keep her temper, she told herself. There was no point in getting angry with Daniel.

He finished off his dessert and pushed the plate aside. 'Would you throw a temper tantrum if Drew got married?' he asked bluntly.

Brodie blinked. 'Is he thinking about it?'

'I have no idea,' he said, but the denial was too smooth. 'You would raise hell with him, wouldn't you? You've got ice cubes in your voice when you even think about it.'

She set her cup down with a firm little click. 'Drew makes his own choices, Daniel. I have nothing to say about what he does with his life.'

'But as long as you're here at Safe Harbour, he can't do as he likes. Isn't it about time he was free?' He pushed his chair back from the table and folded his arms on the linen cloth. 'Drew was twenty-one when Andy died. That's pretty young to be responsible for a little kid. And from what I hear, he's still pulling you out of scrapes. When are you going to grow up, Brodie?'

'I don't believe I'm required to listen to this from you, Daniel.'

'Then you'd better think about it again, dear, I was just as good a friend to your dad as Andy Hammond was. They called us the Three Musketeers when we were young. Not very original, but it gives you the picture.'

'I didn't know that.'

'When John was dying, he brought you back to Hammond's Point because he knew either Andy or I would take care of you. At the time, I was thinking of moving. John wanted you to grow up here, so that meant Andy became your guardian. Many's the time I wished it had been the other way around, for Drew's sake.'

Brodie sipped her coffee. Her lips felt stiff. 'If Drew objected, why didn't he do something about it?'

'Because Drew, my girl, is a very moral man, and he felt an obligation to his father. But don't fool yourself. This has weighed heavily on him. He's counting the days till your birthday, when you'll be out of his care.'

Brodie thought, but Drew said at the party that I could stay here at Safe Harbour as long as I wanted. Did he say that only because he felt he must?

There had been a coolness between them—a distance—since she had come home. She had thought it was her engagement that had caused the problem. But was there more to it than that? Did Drew resent losing the freedom he'd had when she was away at college?

Drew came back in with a smile. 'That's one important problem cleared up,' he said. 'Will you warm my coffee, Brodie?'

Try as she might, she could see nothing in his face that indicated unhappiness. But there had been plenty of it in the last few days. There in the library before dinner, when he told her to stop rubbing his neck, it had been as if he hadn't wanted her to touch him any more.

'Let's go play chess, Daniel. Unless you and Brodie were having an important talk?'

Daniel pushed his chair back. 'We've finished,' he said jovially. 'Now let's see that new strategy of yours, Drew.'

There was nothing worth watching on television, but Brodie sat staring at it anyway. The sitting room was dim, the only light coming from the screen, as she sat there and thought about her problem. Two weeks ago her life had been so well planned out. She would marry Jerry, help him finish school, then be his helper, his companion, his hostess, as he made his career. She would not have hesitated to sink her hopes for success as a singer in order to advance his plans. But now that there was no Jerry, what was she to do?

Drew had said that she was welcome at Safe Harbour. But if she stayed . . .

Was Daniel right? Was her dependence on Drew keeping him from doing as he liked? She had never thought of that before, never considered that Drew's decision to remain a bachelor might have anything to do with her. That was Cynthia's fault. But in any case, it was time for Brodie to grow up.

'I won't continue to be a leech on Drew,' she told herself firmly. 'I have to stop pretending to be the princess of the castle someday, and it might as well be now.'

'Talking to yourself, Bro?' Drew looked in, then went on into his bedroom next door without waiting for an answer. A few minutes later he was back, tossing himself down into his favourite chair with a sigh. 'Good movie?'

'No. It's terrible. How did the chess game go?'

'I was beaten rather badly, but it was a valiant last stand.' He studied her face. 'You look sad, Bro.'

She laughed, without humour. 'You expected me to be dancing across the ceiling?'

'Was it something Daniel said?'

'Does unhappiness have to be caused by anything specific, Drew?' Then, as he waited patiently for an answer, she grumbled, 'I ought to know better than to fence with an attorney. Daniel had a lot to say, yes. He told me that you were tired of being responsible for me.'

Drew frowned. 'It's sweet of Daniel to be so concerned about me. But it's too bad that he isn't more accurate.'

'Are you saying that you aren't anxious to get rid of me? You must be, Drew. Daniel said you were counting the days till I'm twenty-one.' She raised big brown eyes to meet his. 'I don't know why I never thought about your feelings in all this. I guess all these years you've always been there when I needed you, and I never stopped to think about how you must feel about having this helpless little brat on your hands.'

'I haven't felt used, if that's what you mean. And you aren't a brat, Bro.'

'But I can't just take advantage of your good nature forever. You've given up a lot of freedom to take care of me, Drew.'

'It was no sacrifice.'

She didn't look at him as she said quietly, 'Daniel said you're thinking of getting married.'

There was a long silence before he said, finally, 'I guess I'll have to be a little more careful of what I say to Daniel.'

'So it's true.'

'I've considered it. And rejected the idea.'

'Why? Because of me?' Brodie didn't wait for an answer. 'Your wife might not understand the idea of a permanent house guest. You don't need to feel responsible for me any more, Drew. I'm a big girl now. I can take care of myself.'

'You gave real evidence of that when you brought Jerry home,' he pointed out, a hint of sarcasm in his voice. 'It was apparent to anyone with two eyes what Jerry wanted, but if it had been left up to you, Brodie, you'd still be blindly in love.'

She stared at him a long time, and things she had never thought about before began to make sense. Of course Drew hadn't exploded at her announcement, or forbidden her to see Jerry again. He'd played far too much poker in his life—both in and out of a courtroom. He had known that argument would not convince her. So he hadn't argued. He had simply set out to quietly destroy her plans.

'You invited Jerry to play golf with you that day,' she said softly. 'I thought it was strange—that you two were suddenly getting chummy. You made sure that Jerry knew I didn't have a penny, and you did it on purpose, didn't you, Drew?'

His voice was sombre. 'Would you rather I hadn't, Brodie? Would you have preferred to find out after you were married that he was only interested in money?'

She was working herself into an old-fashioned rage, needing desperately to take her anger out on someone. 'You deliberately messed up the only thing I've ever really wanted, Drew!'

'And ruined your life,' he mocked. 'Blame it on me if you must, Bro. I'm handy.'

'I suppose you thought you were being helpful—getting my problems all straightened out. Well, I want to do it on my own. You don't have to count the days any more—they're over!' She stormed towards the door.

His voice caught her in the hallway. 'Be careful, Bro,' he warned grimly. 'Stop and think, or you'll throw away something that means more to you than you will ever understand.'

CHAPTER FOUR

BRODIE juggled the jar of peanut butter and the box of wholewheat crackers in her arms and picked up a package of cheese. It looked so good, but the cellophane wrapping warned that it must be refrigerated, and so she put it back with a sigh. It wasn't easy to choose the kinds of snack foods that she could keep in her room at the residential hotel. And it wasn't very appetising to eat that way, either. But on her present salary, there wasn't much choice. Even meals at the hotel coffee shop added up to more than her budget could afford.

This, she thought, was what poverty felt like. This was what Jerry had been trying to escape. The necessity to watch every penny she spent, the longing for the little extras that she used to buy without a moment's thought—

With Drew's money, she reminded herself, and straightened her shoulders, shaking out the cloud of dark brown hair. It should be a matter of pride, to make it on her own, she told herself. And it wasn't good for a girl's character to remain always in a sheltered environment.

Just the thought of Safe Harbour brought a sharp pain of longing to her stomach. It almost doubled her over, and it took a few moments to get her sense of humour back. At least there was one good thing about living this way, she reminded herself. In two weeks she had lost ten pounds.

She paid for her food and glanced down the street before pushing the door open. Perhaps she was paranoid to keep watching for Drew, she thought. After all, in the two weeks since she had left Safe Harbour she had not heard from him. He'd probably written her off as a spoiled, ungrateful little brat.

And, she admitted, to be perfectly fair, that was exactly what she must have sounded like. She hadn't seen him again after their quarrel that evening. The next day she had hunted out the manager of the only nightclub in town and badgered him into giving her a chance as a performer. Then she had rented a room at the old, rickety railroad hotel—the only thing that approached her price range—and moved a few possessions quietly out of Safe Harbour. She had left Drew a note that thanked him politely for his help over the years, promised rashly to repay the money he'd spent on her, and begged him to leave her alone.

He had. She hadn't even caught a glimpse of him on the street, and he had made no effort to talk to her. He must know where she was; Hammond's Point wasn't big enough to hide in. His indifference must mean that he no longer cared what she did.

Brodie bit her lip. She was glad that he wasn't making a fuss about it, she told herself firmly. But even though she was now doing what she had always wanted, it felt a little lonely to be suddenly without his support.

She stopped by the window of her favourite clothing store, and looked at the coffee- coloured dress on display there. It was a soft, drapy fabric that her fingers longed to touch. Last month she'd have used her allowance to buy it . . .

Stop it, Brodie, she told herself. You're carrying on as if someone had stolen your birthright. Drew had been correct, though; she had been raised in luxury, and it would be difficult to learn to do without all the things that had come so easily before.

With a last longing look at the dress, she walked on. If she bought anything at all right now, it would have to be clothes suitable for the nightclub. She and the manager had had a squabble about that very thing last night.

'This isn't Carnegie Hall,' he'd told her bluntly. 'If you want to keep the customer's attention, you have to give him something to look at.' He'd glanced at her basic black dress with disfavour. 'You're a pretty girl, Brodie. If you'd use a little more make-up . . .'

She smiled, remembering Drew telling her, when she was a teenager, 'You're a pretty girl, Brodie, if you wouldn't hide behind all that make-up.' Funny that two men could look at the same girl and see such different things.

Well, she knew which man's instincts she would trust, Brodie thought, and it wasn't the club manager. All he was interested in was a floor show that would keep the customers coming back. Drew, on the other hand . . . Just what was it about Drew that was so special? she asked herself.

There were people around town who were afraid of him. The combination of aggressive intelligence and inflexible morality made him an opponent to be feared, that was sure. But Brodie had never seen that side of him. The man she knew was warm, compassionate, understanding, generous.

'Hello, Brodie.'

The vibrant voice had been so strongly in her thoughts that for a moment she thought she was imagining it. She turned and looked up at him, startled. 'Drew!' she breathed. He looked like a man without a worry in the world as he stood there, seeming to tower over her, his face tanned, eyes bright.

'How are you, Bro? You're thinner.'

'A little.'

'More than a little,' he pointed out gently. 'Do you like what you're doing?'

She nodded. 'Very much, I like to perform.'

He didn't comment. After a moment, he asked, very softly, 'Are you happy, Bro?'

Was she? She didn't want to spend her life this way, that was sure, but until she got her feet on the ground . . .

He didn't demand that she answer. 'I'll buy you dinner, for old times' sake,' he offered.

'Mrs Riley wouldn't like that,' Brodie murmured.

'It's her day off. Come out to the club with me—we'll play nine holes and then have steaks.'

It sounded so good that her mouth watered. Then she shook her head. 'Don't try to bribe me. I can't, Drew. My show starts in an hour, and I should be getting dressed right now.' She tried to tear herself away, but those slate green eyes were hypnotic. He hadn't touched her, but it felt as if she was chained to the pavement.

Then he shrugged, and the sadness in his eyes wouldn't hide any more. 'I'll see you around, Bro.'

'Sure.' It was barely a whisper as she turned away. Tears blurred her vision as she hurried down the street, back to the safety of her room. She had hurt him—had injured the one person who had never been unkind to her. He might have meddled in her life, but he had never intended to harm her. It was almost more than she could bear, that she had caused Drew pain.

They'd set aside a dressing room for her at the nightclub. That was a fancy name for it, Brodie thought as she checked her appearance in the mirror. 'Closet' would have been a better term. It was so small that she didn't even change clothes there; instead, she dressed in her room at the hotel and walked the two blocks to the nightclub.

She looked herself over thoroughly in the wavy glass of the little mirror, and then, with a sigh, reached for the make-up kit. She couldn't do anything about her clothes, and she wasn't sure she'd want to wear the kind of thing the manager had suggested anyway. But she could put on a bit more eyeliner and mascara. Maybe that would keep him happy.

Her dress was one she had bought for a college dance. It was flattering, and demure, in pale orange, and—the manager was right—it was totally out of place at this club. Well, Brodie thought, if he wanted her to dress differently, he'd have to increase her wages. The way it was she was barely making it. It seemed that every other day she was making a trip to the bank to withdraw a few dollars from her dwindling savings account.

She hoped that the crowd would be a decent one tonight. There had been a bunch of rowdies coming in, the last few nights, heckling her. She didn't quite know what to do, and the manager was no help. He just laughed and said that the teasing was good for her, it helped to loosen her up. Brodie knew that the rowdies were among his best customers. They sat right by the stage, and she could see the debris pile up as the evening wore on—beer cans and overflowing ashtrays and dirty glasses. As for the heckling, she'd have to handle that problem herself. The manager would be of no assistance.

Most of the tables were empty when she started to sing. Many of the patrons were still in the dining room. It was easier to warm up to a small crowd, though, than to walk on to a stage in front of a hundred people.

It would help a great deal, she thought as she walked on to the stage to a smattering of applause, to have a piano backstage. At least then her fingers would be ready when she began to play. But there was no use wishing for the impossible.

She started with some easy things, some modern songs that didn't threaten her vocal range. She was risking her voice, anyway, she knew, with the smoky atmosphere and the lack of a private place to warm up. But a job was a job.

The rowdies came in, partway through the show, and took their regular table. There were only three of them tonight, Brodie saw, but they were the loud ones. Just my luck, she thought irritably.

Another loud group came in almost midway through the show. They took their seats noisily in the centre of the room, and Brodie didn't see who was there till she was halfway through a love song. Then her voice cracked embarrassingly in the middle of a phrase.

Jerry, she thought miserably. She hadn't seen him since the face-to-face in the kitchen at Safe Harbour. And she had to be singing a song that they had listened to together.

It was several moments before her composure returned and she could struggle through the end of the song. Then she got angry. The crowd was noisy tonight, and it was difficult enough to hold a pitch without Jerry being out there, she thought. What on earth had made him come here?

She tried not to look back towards his table, but her eyes were drawn there as if by a magnet. He was in a group, and it took Brodie several minutes to single out the girl he was with. When she did, her fingers stumbled over the keys and she almost stopped playing entirely, for the girl at Jerry's side was Isabel Fanning. Shy little Isabel, who looked as if her greatest dream had come true. She certainly didn't seem nervous tonight.

But then alcohol did that for some people, Brodie thought. She tried to catch Isabel's eye, but the girl was too absorbed in Jerry to even notice Brodie. The rest of the group was staring at her, though, and she saw one of the girls whispering to another behind a manicured hand. Most of these people had been her friends. Brodie wondered uneasily, if they still were. Now that she was no longer living at Safe Harbour, they probably didn't consider her a fit acquaintance.

On her next break the manager called her aside. 'What's the matter with you, Brodie?' he asked angrily. 'You told me you could play the piano. You sound like an amateur out there tonight.'

'The damn piano needs tuning,' she retorted.

'Nobody else has complained.'

'It isn't something you do once in a lifetime, you

know.' She started for her dressing room, but the manager's voice stopped her.

'Listen, Brodie, you're already costing me more than I like to pay. Just how many customers do you think you're bringing in, anyway? I don't see much change from a month ago, and if I'm going to keep paying you you'll have to prove you're worth it.'

'There are a lot of people out there listening to me.'

'Exactly. They're listening, but they aren't drinking enough to pay the rent. There's only one guy I'm positive is here because of you, and one Scotch and soda isn't going to make me a profit tonight.'

Drew was here? But he'd said he was going to play golf ... Don't be silly, Brodie, she told herself. Drew isn't the only man in Hammond's Point who drinks Scotch and soda.

'Watch your step, Brodie, or you'll be looking for a job again,' the manager added.

She paused beside the table where Jerry and Isabel sat and shook her head at an invitation from one of the men to join them. 'But you just started to sing,' Isabel said. 'You're already taking a break?'

'I'll be back in a few minutes,' Brodie told her. 'I'm sorry about having to cancel your invitation to tea, by the way.'

Isabel shrugged. 'We can get together another time. But it won't be at Safe Harbour, will it?' She went off into a fit of giggles.

Brodie bit her tongue. It was painfully obvious that the girl had had too much to drink. She supposed that it was Jerry's doing. He looked a little the worse for wear himself.

Her dressing room, tiny as it was, would be a haven of peace for a few minutes. She needed the time to get herself ready for the second half of the show.

But she wasn't to have the opportunity. Her Scotch-drinking customer was Drew, after all. She spotted him at a back corner table, alone, sipping his drink. He raised a casual hand, and when she came over to his table, he stood up. 'Would you like to join me?'

'Why are you here, Drew?' she asked curtly.

He held her chair and lazily sat down again. 'I wanted to see your show.'

'I thought you were going to play golf.'

'I did. Halfway through the front nine, I suddenly got the feeling I should be here instead. Silly of me, isn't it?'

'Now that you've seen the show, I'm certain you have some comments about it.'

'I'm not sure you want to hear them,' he warned.

'I'm a professional now. I can take it.'

'All right. The show stinks, Brodie,' he said flatly. 'You aren't cut out to be a nightclub singer.'

She bristled. 'And you're some kind of authority?'

'No. That's the horrible thing about it. It doesn't take a music critic to see it.' Then, more gently, 'Your voice is fine. But what you're trying to do with it doesn't fit.'

'Thanks for your generous help,' she snapped.

'Anytime. You don't belong here, Bro.'

'As the manager told me, it isn't Carnegie Hall. But we can't all start at the top.'

'By the time you get out of here, you may not have any voice left.'

'I'll take my chances. I have to get back on stage now.'

Drew didn't comment. He just stood up politely as she left the table. A few minutes later she noticed that he had left the club.

She had no set programme, and she found herself in the second half wandering from one old favourite to another, many of them things she had sung with Drew. Darn him anyhow, she thought, as she began the accompaniment for a more modern song. Keep up the old-fashioned stuff and she'd be out of a job before the night was over.

The rowdies were drinking heavily tonight. Several times they interrupted her performance to try to buy

Brodie drinks. They'd never been so loud before, and by the time the show was finished she was shaking from irritation and anger.

She retreated to her dressing room as if it were a sanctuary, and sat there for a long time, listening to the pounding of the juke box through the thin walls, trying to figure out what she could do to hold this act together. She had no delusions about her chances—she knew the odds of success as a singer were heavily against her—but she couldn't just walk away.

Besides, she thought bleakly, what could she do? If she gave up on this act, what was left?

The city lights were dim down in this part of town. Brodie thought, as she left the sheltered back door of the nightclub, that she would never get used to walking by herself down here. The dark had a different quality up on the hill, where Safe Harbour stood. There it was a warm blanket snuggling down around the houses. Down here in the valley it was a fearsome creature to be beaten back.

'And your imagination is going to get you into trouble, Brodie, my girl,' she told herself with wry humour. She almost wished that she had picked up a chair to carry with her—just to keep the darkness at bay.

A burst of laughter came from the parking lot as she passed through it on her way to the hotel, and Brodie shivered. Sometimes she was afraid of the people who frequented the nightclub. Sometimes she even thought she could hear footsteps behind her on the street . . .

'And sometimes you're afraid of your shadow, too,' she mocked herself, trying to laugh away her fright. But she increased her pace anyway.

Another burst of laughter, and Brodie's heart started to race. This wasn't imagination. She risked a glance over her shoulder and saw the three rowdies who had been so much trouble tonight. They were half a block behind her, and the nominal safety of the hotel was two blocks ahead.

'Hey, honey!' one of them called. 'How's about a little drink, now that you're off duty?'

Brodie thought about breaking into a run, but she was already walking as fast as she could in those absurdly high heels. She couldn't possibly outrun them, and there were no other people in sight. Grimly, she ignored them and focused on the dingy sign above the hotel's front door. She had to get there first, she simply had to . . .

A hand on her arm brought a strangled scream to her lips. 'Well, now, isn't she a pretty baby, up close?' It was the ringleader. His other hand stretched out towards the dark hair loose about her shoulders. 'Soft as a cloud,' he said, with a note of wonder in his voice. 'How about a little kiss, Brodie?'

'Leave me alone,' she said. She tried to keep her voice firm, but there was a telltale tremble.

'Just a little kiss for Max won't hurt you, pretty baby,' he wheedled.

Brodie stared up at him in horror as he bent his head, and beer fumes seemed to close in on her.

'You have to learn to be nice to the customers,' he pointed out.

Panic gave her strength, and she pushed him away.

His eyes narrowed. 'What's the matter?' he asked, and his hand tightened on her arm till pain shot through her. 'Something wrong with me? We'll see about whether I get my kiss or not.' The teasing humour was gone from his voice, and raw fear choked Brodie's throat.

'Let her go, Max.' The firm voice cut through the haze that seemed to surround her.

The hand on Brodie's arm didn't loosen. 'Well, if it isn't the Perry Mason of Hammond's Point,' the ringleader's jeering voice said. 'Do you want to join the fun?'

Drew took a step closer. 'It won't be a joke any more if Miss McKenzie files assault and battery charges, Max. You're still on probation, aren't you? I don't think your parole officer will see much humour in another court appearance.' His voice was calm.

Max's hand dropped to his side. 'All right, Hammond, you made your point,' he growled. 'All I was doing was teasing the lady, but I know better than to push it. It would be your word against mine, and I don't want to go back up the river.'

'You're a wise man, Max. Come here, Brodie.'

She huddled in Drew's shadow, too frightened yet to have regained her voice.

Max and his two companions faded off down a nearby alley. The two other bullies hadn't said a word through the entire encounter.

Brodie started to tremble violently. She clung to Drew's arm for the next block. When they reached the hotel, she said, 'Thanks, Drew.' It was a feeble croak.

'I'm coming up.'

'I can't take a man to my room!'

'This hotel has no security. There could be any number of thugs waiting for you in the hallway.'

She shuddered and didn't argue any more. Every shadow she saw on the dimly lighted stairs seemed to hide another Max, leering out at her.

On the third floor, she unlocked the door of her dingy room and turned to him. 'I won't be so careless again, Drew. Thanks for rescuing me.'

His mouth twisted. 'And just how are you going to take precautions? Call a cab to bring you three blocks? And what are you going to do about these dark halls? What if Max is waiting for you here tomorrow?' Drew pushed the door open and followed her in.

'You can't be in here, Drew,' she pointed out. 'The hotel's rules . . .'

'And who's going to stop me?' he asked. 'That's the whole point. Dammit, Brodie, don't you understand the danger you're in?' He gave the door a shove, and then bent to examine the flimsy lock.

When he looked up at Brodie, his eyes dark with exasperation, she shrugged. 'Nobody who lives here has anything worth stealing,' she pointed out flippantly.

He didn't laugh at the feeble joke.

'Drew, come on. Stop trying to scare me.' The episode out on the street was beginning to feel like only a bad dream.

'All right,' he said. 'You know I wouldn't hurt you. Or do you, Brodie?' He twisted the lock and turned to her, and the set look on his face startled her. 'But what if I wasn't good old Drew, Brodie? What if I followed you up here with other intentions?'

He was advancing on her steadily, and Brodie backed away across the room. She stumbled over a discarded shoe and almost fell, catching herself with difficulty. 'Drew,' she breathed, 'don't be ridiculous!'

He raised a sardonic eyebrow and didn't stop stalking her. 'What's ridiculous about it? I'm a man, and you're a very pretty young woman, and you've just spent the evening singing a lot of sexy songs for me. What could be more natural than for me to want you?'

There was nowhere left for her to run. Brodie had flattened herself against the wall, and she closed her eyes, trying to deny the nightmare she found herself trapped in. This isn't really happening, she thought, it isn't really Drew who is here—Drew wouldn't say those things to me, or think those things . . .

'And if I want to kiss you, Brodie,' the inexorable voice went on, so close to her ear that it seemed he was inside her head, 'or rape you, or murder you—who is going to stop me?'

She choked on a shuddery breath.

His fingertip traced the outline of her face, pushing the dark hair back, following the line of her cheekbone and the delicate hollow under it. His breath was hot against her skin. Then he bent suddenly and picked her up.

Brodie's heart jolted painfully against her ribs; she could hardly breathe.

My God, she thought. This can't be happening. Not Drew——

He put her gently down on the bed, his hand stroking the length of her sable-brown hair as it tumbled out of the neat twist.

'You are so flaming beautiful,' he said, and his voice was husky.

She was terrified by this darkly threatening Drew, but she knew that there was no escape. Even if she screamed, no one would interfere. She closed her eyes tightly, trying to shut him out.

'Dammit, Bro, have I made my point?' He sounded cross, like a teacher whose pupil was slow at catching on.

She gasped for breath, and relief at the sudden change in the tone of his voice washed over her like the incoming tide. 'Oh, my God, you scared me, Drew,' she whimpered. She opened tear-wet eyes, sat up, and smiled up at him. 'I thought for a minute you meant it.'

'If I have to shake sense into you, I' will,' he threatened, and his hands closed on her upper arms.

Brodie pulled away from him, and his eyes fell on the red marks left on her arm by Max's hand.

Drew's whole face seemed to twist in pain. 'If I'd been just a couple of minutes earlier,' he muttered under his breath, 'that wouldn't have happened. I'd like to kill him for doing that to you.'

She brushed tears off her cheek and smiled mistily. 'It's all right, Drew. It won't even bruise.' She let her fingers trail down across his tanned face. 'Thank you for caring about what happens to me,' she said softly, and leaned forward to kiss him lightly on the cheek, the kind of kiss she had given him hundreds of times before.

He seemed to freeze for an instant under the gentle

caress, and as she drew back, he stared down at her, his dark eyes questioning.

She didn't suspect what he was about to do until he bent his head to kiss her. She couldn't have moved, anyway, for she was half-sitting on the bed, and Drew's body blocked any escape. But even if she could have avoided the caress, she wouldn't have. Just a brotherly kiss, she thought.

He tasted her lips gently, and she found herself responding almost unaware as his fingers slid up into the long strands of her hair, cupping her head to hold her mouth against his. Each touch of his mouth drained strength from her until she was clinging to him for support. Then he released her lips slowly, unwillingly, to nibble at the velvet skin of her cheek, and finally, with a long sigh, he let her go. 'Bro?' he said huskily.

'I think you'd better go home, Drew.' Her voice was a bit breathless. And I'd better get out of this bed, she thought, or anything might happen.

'Do you need to take anything with you tonight? Or can we pick it all up tomorrow?'

'What do you mean?' She turned in the centre of the room, puzzled by his question.

'I'm taking you home to Safe Harbour, that's what. Come on, Bro. Get your things.'

She shook her head firmly. 'I'm not going. This is my home now.'

'Brodie, be sensible. You aren't safe here.'

'Yes, you've proved that,' she agreed.

'You can't mean that you're afraid of me?' There was a long silence. 'I'm sorry. I didn't mean to frighten you—just to make you realise the danger you've put yourself in.'

Brodie shrugged. 'You didn't frighten me,' she said, and was uneasily aware that it wasn't quite the truth. 'Just go away, Drew.'

He pushed the hair back from his forehead with a

shaky hand and stared down at her. 'I would never hurt you, Brodie . . .'

'Get out.' Her voice was a hoarse croak. She braced herself against the wall and stared at him.

'Come with me.' He reached for her hand, and Brodie snatched it away.

'Don't touch me,' she snapped and turned away.

There was a long silence. 'We'll talk about it tomorrow,' he said. 'Prop a chair under the door handle as soon as I leave, Bro.'

She did. From the window she could see his car, parked on the side street, and she watched morosely as it pulled away from the kerb. Home to Safe Harbour, she thought, and flung herself across the old bedspread.

My God, she thought. He was threatening to rape me, and half of me didn't want him to stop.

'Cheap,' she told herself aloud. 'That's what you are, Brodie McKenzie. You're cheap.'

Jerry, she thought. Why did things have to go so wrong?

CHAPTER FIVE

JERRY was at the club the next night. He was alone this time, and he sat towards the back, in the shadows. But Brodie knew he was there, and she knew that his eyes never left her during the first half of the show. It was agony to have him watching her. What had brought him there, anyway, she wondered bitterly. He'd certainly made it plain enough that he had no further interest in her.

But she loved him, and that didn't make it easier to deal with his presence. Her heart still felt raw from the harsh words he had flung at her that day in the kitchen at Safe Harbour, and she still shivered with fear when she remembered how he would have struck her if Drew had not intervened.

Drew. Just thinking about him sent cold chills through her body. She was horrified by her behaviour last night. She had been so hungry for someone to love her and care about her, even if that someone wasn't Jerry, that she had responded to Drew as if he had been a long-absent lover. At least that was how she had explained it to herself, in the long hours before she had fallen into an exhausted, restless sleep.

And then, each footstep in the hall, each creak of the old hotel, and Brodie had been wide awake. She was so tired now that she could hardly keep her eyes on the music, and she wasn't even sure whether her voice was trembling from exhaustion, or if it was her imagination.

In fact, the only thing that was going right was that the table directly in front of the stage, the one that had been occupied by Max and his friends on so many nights, was conspicuously empty tonight. At least she wouldn't have them to cope with as she walked back to the hotel, she thought as she closed the first half of the show.

But then, of course, she wouldn't have Drew to watch over her, either. The club's patrons were scattered through the big cabaret room, but her careful survey of the crowd could not have missed him.

Brodie wondered drearily if he was having as many regrets today as she was.

She would have passed Jerry's table—she had to, to reach her dressing room—with nothing more than a cool smile. But he rose, a little unsteadily, and indicated the chair across from him. Brodie didn't sit down, but she paused. 'Hello, Jerry.'

'So he kicked you out anyway.' Jerry's voice held a note of challenge.

His tie was loose, she noticed, and his eyes were bleary, as if he had had a great deal to drink. She didn't answer his question.

'He wasn't satisfied to get rid of me,' Jerry went on. 'You were wrong about what your dear, precious Drew would put up with, weren't you?'

His face was flushed, and when she still didn't answer, he said, louder, 'Sit down, Brodie. Let's have a little talk.'

Brodie shook her head. 'There's nothing to talk about, Jerry. You didn't leave anything undiscussed last time.'

'I love you, Bro. It was a mistake.'

'What was? Falling in love with me before you'd made sure I was able to support you?' Her voice was low and tight. She tried to brush past him.

He caught her arm. 'I said, sit down. And I meant it.'

She looked down at his hand, and said coldly, 'Don't ever touch me again, Jerry.'

For a moment they stood there, staring at each other, and then Brodie brushed his hand off her arm and walked on, briskly, to her dressing room.

She sat down on the rickety folding chair and put her

head into her hands. Pride had carried her through the hardest moment, letting her walk out of the room with her head high and her spine straight. But as soon as she was out of his sight, pride had fled, leaving raw pain throbbing through her body.

'I will never see him again,' she whispered. It wasn't all a nightmare, after all. Somewhere, vaguely, in the back of her mind, she had thought that someday they would be together. Someday they would look back from a rosily-happy future—on an anniversary, perhaps—and laugh at this misunderstanding over a glass of champagne.

But now she had to face the reality. They would not have a future at all, not together. It was over, and she could deceive herself no longer.

But love didn't die so easily. Even Drew had admitted that the first love was never really forgotten. And Drew should know. It had been years since Cynthia had jilted him. It didn't matter to Drew that Cynthia had been unworthy of him, Brodie thought. He still loved her, and no other woman would ever take her place in his heart. And it didn't matter with Jerry, either. He might be calculating and determined to take care of himself at all costs, but he was Brodie's first love.

'Brodie?' the manager said tartly, banging on the dressing room door. 'If it isn't too much trouble, do you suppose you could finish your show?'

She jumped up, banging her head against the low, slanted ceiling. 'Sorry, I didn't watch the time.'

He grunted. 'You'd better start paying attention.' There was dire warning in his voice.

Brodie rubbed the sore spot on her scalp and pulled the door open. It was becoming increasingly difficult to walk on to that stage.

She took a deep breath and walked out to face the crowd again.

*   *   *

In the close confinement of the little dressing room, it was hard to pull the long dress off. Brodie had to wriggle out of it, and by that time the dress was badly in need of pressing. She pulled on jeans and trainers and pushed the dress into her duffle bag. At least tonight she would be able to run if she had to.

Darn Drew, anyhow. All that talk last night of hooligans lurking, waiting to attack her, had left her ready to scream at shadows. And there were plenty of them to scream at tonight, she thought grimly as she stood for a minute at the back door of the club. The wind had picked up, heralding a summer thunderstorm, and clouds played hopscotch with the moon, sending huge, weird shadows wheeling across the streets.

I hate thunderstorms, Brodie thought, and then admitted to the truth—she was afraid of them. She squared her shoulders determinedly and took the first step out of the doorway. It's time to grow up, my girl, she added to herself. There isn't a Safe Harbour for shelter now.

A car engine purred to life in the far corner of the parking lot, and Brodie shuddered. 'And you'd jump a mile if a mouse squeaked right now, too,' she mocked herself, and ignored it. The rowdies hadn't turned up at the club at all. Drew had frightened them off last night.

She took a deep breath of the suddenly cool air. It smelled so good after the stale tobacco smoke of the nightclub. Behind her, over the roar of the wind, she thought she could hear a car engine. I'm being followed, she thought, and panic began to rise in her throat. If it was Max, again——

You're only imagining it, Brodie, she told herself firmly.

The lights of a tavern in the next block spilled out across the sidewalk. As she passed it the door opened to a wave of laughter and two men came out.

She dodged them, and one stopped, reeling a little, and said, 'Well, if it isn't the little songbird.'

It was one of the rowdies who had remained silent the night before, while Max threatened her. Brodie kept walking, but her heart was pounding.

'I'm not on probation, honey,' he added, 'so Hammond's threats won't get in our way. Want to have some fun?'

She kept silent and dodged the man's outstretched hand.

A door slammed. She hadn't been imagining the car after all. She started to run, her sneakers pounding on the pavement along with the first enormous drops of rain as the storm broke. She couldn't hear the car motor any more, but she ran on, choking for breath, dragging air into her protesting lungs.

The hotel had never looked so dark or grim. And yet that was the only safety she had. She had almost reached the door when a hand closed on her arm. She tried to scream, but the sound caught in her throat. She swung around with horror in her eyes, and looked up into Drew's face.

'It was you, following me?' she breathed.

'I didn't mean to frighten you. I just wanted to be certain you got here safely.'

She looked up at him for a long moment, and then she flung herself into his arms, sobbing out her relief like the frightened child she was.

The rain hissed down from the angry sky, and in seconds they were wet through. Drew pushed Brodie into the hotel lobby. 'Would you like me to walk you to your room?' he asked gently.

She looked around at the old, dank lobby, paper peeling from the walls, sections of plaster gone from the ceiling, old vinyl furniture spitting its stuffing over the ragged carpet. And she thought, If I have to spend one more night in this place I will surely go mad.

'Take me home, Drew,' she whispered. 'I want to go home to Safe Harbour.'

His whole body seemed to relax. 'Sure, Bro. Let's get your things.'

She shook her head fiercely. 'I'll pick them up tomorrow. I don't want to stay here another minute.'

The Lincoln was dark and quiet, and Brodie put her head back against the leather upholstery with a sigh. The rain was falling in torrents now, and lightning cut through the sky. Brodie shuddered.

'Are you scared?' He started the motor, but she couldn't hear it over the roar of the falling rain. The wipers could scarcely keep up as they struggled valiantly with the sheets of water pouring down over the glass.

'Not a Safe Harbour,' Brodie said. There was a tremor in her voice as she caught sight of the big house on the hill.

'There is nothing magical about that house, Bro,' he said quietly. The car swung into the driveway, where rain still pounded on the concrete. Once inside the garage, they sat silently in the car until the roar of waterdrops on the slate roof died to a trickle.

'Let me go ahead and unlock the back door,' Drew suggested.

Brodie shook her head. 'I can't get any wetter,' she pointed out. And besides, she thought, I can't wait another instant to feel the comfort of Safe Harbour around me.

Her hand found the kitchen light switch, and she laughed for the first time in days as she got a good look at Drew. 'You look like something they just rescued from the river,' she giggled.

'You're no Miss Universe yourself at the moment. Here, have a towel so you don't drip on Mrs Riley's floor on your way to the shower.'

Brodie blotted her dripping hair. 'We need to talk, Drew.'

'After you have a hot shower.' He was wiping rivulets of water off his arms.

'I never catch cold,' Brodie protested, but she obediently climbed the stairs to her own room.

Nothing had changed, of course. She hadn't expected that it would have, though Drew could very well have stored all of her belongings in the attic and called in the decorators to help him forget that she had ever lived there. She rummaged through the closet for an old terry bathrobe and stripped off her dripping clothes.

Drew was waiting in the upstairs sitting room when she came in, rosy from the hot shower, her hair wrapped turban-style in a towel.

'What do you want to talk to me about, Brodie?'

She curled up in the chair across from his. 'What I'm going to do,' she said confidingly.

He raised an eyebrow. 'I assumed you were going to stay here.'

'Oh, I am! I mean, I'd like to. But on my terms, Drew. I don't want to take advantage of you, and I'm not a child any more.'

'I'll concede that,' he said with a wry smile, and his eyes slid slowly over the slim figure in the bathrobe before returning to her face.

Brodie was a little uneasy, but she pushed on. 'I want to pay for my room and board. I can't afford very much—not nearly enough, I know. But I want to give you what I was paying at the hotel. And——'

He said, between gritted teeth, 'This is your home, Brodie. You will not pay to live here.'

'Then I'll move out.' Their eyes met and locked.

Drew swore under his breath. 'To another luxurious place like the hotel?'

'I'm going to be responsible for myself, Drew.' Her voice was firm.

'Brodie——' He ran a hand through his hair, and it stood up in wet brown peaks. 'All right. You win. You can pay rent for your room. Is that everything?'

'Not entirely. There's the question of my food.'

'Good God, Bro, you have to eat!' he exploded. 'What difference does it make if you share my table?'

'It makes a lot of difference to me,' she said, with

quiet dignity. 'I want to feel as if I'm earning my keep, Drew.'

'And just how do you propose to do that?' he asked warily.

'I'll help Mrs Riley in the kitchen. She could use an extra hand. And when she has a day off, I can take over the cooking.'

'Damn it, Bro, I will not stand for you being a kitchen maid.'

'I am no longer a guest here. I am here because it is convenient for me, and I expect to pay for that convenience.'

There was a long silence while he studied her. 'You aren't going to back down, are you, Brodie?'

'No. Take it or leave it.'

'And if I leave it?'

'Then I'll move back to the hotel tomorrow morning. You don't want that, do you, Drew?'

'You tempt me,' he admitted. 'Very well, Bro. You win. You can start tomorrow morning. It's Mrs Riley's day off.'

'She was off yesterday,' Brodie said, startled.

'And today,' he agreed. 'Her grandchildren came to visit her.'

'Oh.'

'That's the way it goes. Take it or leave it,' he mocked gently.

'All right,' she said bravely. 'Breakfast at seven-thirty?'

'Better make it seven,' he recommended. 'I have to be at the office early.'

It was half-past six when Brodie came down the stairs, her eyes barely open. She had intended to be down at least an hour earlier, but her body, exhausted from the previous night without sleep, had different ideas. Now she was late.

She surveyed Mrs Riley's spotless kitchen with

foreboding, and then said, 'How bad can it be, Bro? You put the bacon in the skillet and turn the heat on. How complicated can that get?'

Well, the first thing was the coffee. Once it was started, she could concentrate on things like eggs and toast. She poured hot water into the percolator to hurry the process along and read the instructions on the side of the coffee can. Measuring out ten spoonfuls of coffee seemed like a lot of bother, so she just dumped grounds into the basket, looked at it judiciously, and added a little more. One thing Drew hated was weak coffee. She plugged the percolator in and looked in the refrigerator.

When he came down the stairs, the bacon was popping wickedly in the skillet, sending grease flying all over. An egg was bouncing in a saucepan full of boiling water, and Brodie was concentrating on making the toaster give up the slices of bread that it was apparently holding hostage.

Her hair was sliding out of the ribbon she had carelessly tied around it, she was already hot and irritable, and she was ready to swear. Drew, on the other hand, looked cool and comfortable in a light grey summer suit, the jacket still slung over his arm. He put it down on the counter, a safe distance from the bacon, and reached for a coffee cup. 'Good morning, Brodie,' he said cheerfully.

She tried to blow a lock of hair out of her eyes and finally pryed half a slice of toast free. 'Morning,' she said. 'Your breakfast will be ready soon.'

Drew was looking thoughtfully into the depths of his cup. It was a full minute before he raised green eyes to meet hers, and then he glanced at the stove. 'How long,' he asked gingerly, 'has my egg been in that water?'

'About ten minutes,' she said, and gave him a defiant look. 'You did say you wanted breakfast at seven, and you're late.'

'I see.' He carried the cup over to the breakfast bar and sat down. He sipped the coffee, reached for the sugar bowl, and put in three heaping teaspoons. 'Shall we get it out before it explodes?'

Brodie glared at him and spooned the egg into a china egg cup. She set it in front of him along with the half-slice of toast. 'The bread was frozen this morning, and it stuck in the toaster,' she said, daring him to make a comment.

Drew tapped his spoon on the egg, which gave no sign of cracking. He sighed and put the spoon down. Brodie turned back to the stove just in time to see the bacon give off wisps of smoke. She grabbed for the fork, but by the time she'd pulled the strips of meat out of the pan, they were almost black.

'I don't suppose you want bacon,' she said.

'I believe I'll pass, thank you,' Drew said gravely and added another spoonful of sugar to his coffee. He sat stirring it and watching Brodie as she struggled with the toaster.

'Bro?' he said gently. 'I have a lunch date with a client. And as for tonight—why don't I bring Chinese food home? You always liked that.'

The other slice of bread slid out of the toaster just then, and Brodie threw it at him. He ducked and the toast splattered over the countertop.

She braced her hands on the edge of the countertop and fought off tears.

'I'm sorry,' Drew said finally. He pushed his coffee cup aside and came across the kitchen.

'What for? I'm the one who messed everything up.' She wouldn't look at him.

His hand brushed gently down her tumbled hair. 'I'll call you later, all right?'

'Don't be late tonight. I have to be at the club by eight.'

He looked unhappy, but he didn't comment. A couple of minutes later she heard the Lincoln purr down the driveway.

'I am not going to cry,' she told herself firmly, as her

chin wobbled. She got a cup down, filled it with coffee, and went to sit down for a minute, looking around at the unholy mess she'd made of the kitchen.

'And it looked so easy,' she murmured.

The dark brown liquid was unbearably bitter. She stared at it for a minute, and then pushed the cup aside with a careless hand. She put her head down in her folded arms on the edge of the breakfast bar and started to sob.

She didn't know how long she'd indulged her self-pity before a horrified voice at the back door said, 'My God, what happened to my kitchen?'

Brodie looked up in shock, tears still streaming down her face. 'What are you doing here?' she asked blankly.

Mrs Riley set her handbag down on the counter. 'My grandchildren went home early, thank heaven. At least, I thought it was wonderful till I saw this mess. When did you come home? And what happened to my kitchen?'

'I fixed Drew's breakfast,' Brodie said sullenly.

Mrs Riley started to laugh. 'Dry your tears and tell me all about it.'

Brodie did. Mrs Riley started to pour herself some coffee, took one look at the colour of it, and then emptied the percolator's contents down the drain. 'I hope that stuff doesn't destroy the pipes,' she said thoughtfully. 'So you're going to help me out, to earn your board?'

'That's about it.'

'I'm glad you showed enough sense to come home. It's been very quiet around here, and you could use a little fattening up. You can start by putting the rest of that food down the garbage disposal, and we'll fix you a real breakfast.'

Brodie collected the remains. 'How do you do it?' she asked curiously. 'How do you know when he's coming down, so everything is ready?'

'I don't.'

'What does that mean?'

'Mr Hammond was teasing you, Brodie. He's fixed his own breakfast for two years, ever since you went off to school. He said it was pointless for me to come in early, just to make a pot of coffee and a slice of toast.'

'And I fixed eggs and bacon——' Brodie was outraged.

'I seldom come to work before nine,' Mrs Riley added.

Brodie fed the hardboiled egg down the disposal. 'I never knew that.'

'Of course not,' Mrs Riley said gently. 'You never get up till after nine, when you're home at all.'

Brodie let that one pass. It was true enough, after all. 'Will you teach me?' she asked. 'I didn't know it could be so difficult.'

'You have talked yourself into a spot, haven't you, Brodie? Sure, I'll teach you. Let's start with the coffee. You always use cold water . . .'

'I'm still not sure I can do it,' Brodie said. She felt as if her head had been stuffed with facts, and she was afraid that at the critical moment every bit of knowledge would flee.

'Of course you can,' Mrs Riley said robustly. 'The baked potatoes are already in the oven, and nobody can mess up sour cream with chives. You've already made the salads and the vegetable tray. The only thing left to do is the steaks, and if you put them under the grill for precisely five minutes on a side—absolutely no more than that—Mr Hammond's T-bone will be exactly the way he likes it.' She pulled her apron off and hung it in the pantry.

'Why are you doing this?' Brodie asked curiously.

Mrs Riley grinned. 'I'm not above wanting to see him get his comeuppance. I just wish I could be here to see his face, but that would ruin the effect.'

'No, if you were here he'd never believe I did it.'

'That's right—and remember it. You did do every step in preparing this dinner. And even if it is a simple menu, you deserve credit. That's why I'm leaving.'

'Can't you wait a little while? Let me rehearse one more time?' Brodie's voice was panicky.

Mrs Riley shook her head. 'No. He might come home any minute now. You'll be fine. You were wonderful on the 'phone, convincing him to give you another chance, weren't you?'

'That's different,' Brodie said gloomily. 'Words are easy.'

She sat at the breakfast bar, drinking coffee and watching the steaks where they lay on the butcher block, warming up to room temperature, as if they might disappear under her eyes. And she felt like a condemned prisoner walking to the gallows when she heard the Lincoln purr into the drive.

The garage door slammed, and Drew came into the kitchen, whistling.

'If you'd like a drink before dinner, there's a pitcher of Margaritas in the refrigerator,' she said.

He reached for a glass. 'Want one?'

'No, thanks,' Brodie said grimly. 'I'm cooking.'

Drew kept a straight face with an effort, and asked, 'Do I have time for a shower? The air conditioning went out at the office today.'

'Sure. It'll just take a few minutes to cook the steaks.'

'Give me ten and I'll be ready.' He glanced at the steaks, as if, Brodie thought resentfully, he thought the next time he saw them they'd be charred. Then he leaned against the refrigerator and thoughtfully sipped his Margarita. 'I thought you'd jump at the chance to eat out tonight, Bro.'

'I made a promise, Drew,' she said firmly. 'And I'm going to keep it if it kills both of us.'

He looked doubtful, as if he thought it might cost a life or two. Then he shrugged. 'I'll be down soon.'

'Take your time,' Brodie said cordially. 'I've already learned not to start cooking till I see you.'

Drew pushed his plate aside with a satisfied sigh, leaned back in his chair, and said, 'Okay, Brodie. Out with it.'

She looked at him innocently, brown eyes wide. 'What do you mean? Would you like dessert? It's only peach sherbet from the supermarket, but . . .'

'No, thanks. I don't want anything to remove the taste of that steak. I'd have sworn you had never cooked a steak in your life, Bro.'

'There is a lot you don't know about me, Drew.' She sipped her coffee (quite good, she noted, if she did have to say so herself) and tried to look mysterious.

'Where did you learn?'

'Have you never heard of cookbooks?'

He looked her over at length and then pushed his chair back. 'You aren't going to tell me, are you? Very well. I'll take care of the dishes, since you did the cooking.'

Brodie didn't move. 'Tell the truth, Drew. You intended to sneak out for a sandwich as soon as I left for the nightclub, didn't you?'

'To be honest, I thought I'd have to. I wouldn't want to die of starvation; it's so dreadfully slow. Go get dressed and I'll take you to work.'

'That's a lot of bother for you.'

'And how do you plan to get there, Bro? It's a bit too far to walk, now.'

'I hadn't thought about it.'

'As long as you're working there, I'll take you down and pick you up.'

She started to protest, and he came around the table and leaned over her. His eyes were dark, and she thought for an uneasy moment that he intended to kiss her. But that had been just a fluke, she told herself. It wouldn't happen again.

He just stood there, his hand warm on the delicate

line of her cheek. 'Brodie? There are very few things I
do just because I have to. And this isn't one of them.
Remember that, all right? It will save us both a great
deal of trouble.'

CHAPTER SIX

THE coffee-coloured dress looked even better on Brodie than it had a week before in the window of the little dress shop. She fought a swift battle with her conscience, and surrendered. She didn't really need the dress, but moving back to Safe Harbour had relaxed her budget a bit. And she deserved something nice to raise her spirits, if only because she was due at the nightclub in fifteen minutes to have a talk with the boss. What he was going to tell her, she didn't know, but she suspected she wasn't going to like it.

With that justification in mind, she paid over the cash and put the dress box under her arm with a sense of satisfaction. Now, she thought, whatever the boss wants to talk about, I'll feel better about it.

The cabaret that was so dim and intimate in the evenings looked as big as a barn in the light of day, and the stage looked tiny at one end. The air still looked hazy, and the scent of stale cigarette smoke would never entirely disappear. Brodie walked quickly through, wanting to spend as little time there as possible, and tapped on the manager's office door.

He was smoking a cigar, and he leaned back in his chair and propped his feet up when she came in. 'Sit down, Brodie,' he ordered.

She did, carefully balancing the dress box on her lap. 'What did you want to talk to me about?'

He chewed the cigar and looked her over thoughtfully. 'When you came in three weeks ago and asked for this job, you put a salary figure on yourself that was a lot steeper than I wanted to pay.'

'And we negotiated a compromise,' Brodie pointed out.

79

'Which is still higher than I usually pay for an entertainer. But I agreed to give you a chance.'

Brodie watched, fascinated, as he moved the cigar from one corner of his mouth to the other without using his hand.

'You aren't paying your way, Brodie. I haven't come close to breaking even on your salary.' He didn't sound unkind, just factual. 'I can't afford to keep you full-time. Now if you came in once a month, maybe you could draw enough of a crowd to make it worthwhile.'

'I can't live on that kind of money,' Brodie argued.

He shrugged. 'That's not my problem. I'm not running the Salvation Army here, you know. Or if you'd like to switch jobs, I can use another waitress on the evening shift.'

She could already hear what Drew would have to say about that. And as far as Brodie was concerned, he never would hear it. If the group of rowdies wouldn't leave her alone on stage, she shuddered to think what would happen if she was serving them drinks.

'No, thanks. I'm a singer, not a barmaid.'

He shrugged and chewed the cigar. 'It's your choice. Let me know if you want to work once a month or so.' He put his feet on the floor and reached for the newspaper. 'As for you being a singer, Brodie, there's some different opinions about that, too. If you can't make it work in Hammond's Point, I wouldn't recommend you tackle the big time.' He opened the paper, concealing his face behind it.

She had been dismissed. Well, Brodie thought irritably as she left the club, with its sour smell of smoke and spilled beer, thank heaven there were more places than Hammond's Point in the world! If she had to depend on people like these for her audience, it was hardly worth the trouble.

The manager's words rang in her ears. 'If you can't make it work in Hammond's Point——'

Brodie shook her head angrily, trying to drive his words out of her mind. That's not the problem, she thought. It isn't that I'm not good enough, it's that this town just isn't big enough to support a singer. Or it was the act—if I'd just had time to work on the act——

She caught her reflection in a store window, and was shocked at the rage that twisted her face. For a moment there, she was almost ugly, and she walked on in a chastened mood.

Just who are you angry at, Bro? she asked herself. The manager? No, because he's just doing his job. The people of Hammond's Point? No, because they aren't obliged to sit in a bar and buy drinks if they don't like the entertainment.

'You're angry with yourself, Bro,' she muttered. 'Because you tried for your dream, and you flopped. You haven't got the stuff to make it as an entertainer, and it's about time you faced it.'

The manager was right, after all. If her little act could do no more than wobble along from night to night in Hammond's Point, what chance would she have against the competition in a bigger town?

It hurt to admit it, but there it was. She might as well face up to it now.

She walked slowly up the hill towards Safe Harbour, and decided to stop at Drew's office to see what he'd like for dinner. Mrs Riley was back to her regular work schedule, and this was her day off. Brodie was almost beginning to enjoy the routine; she'd done much of the cooking in the last week, after Mrs Riley's careful eye, and she felt a growing confidence in her ability.

The law office was cool and plush, with its hardwood panelling and deep carpets and tasteful paintings. The quiet interior reflected not only the firm's reputation, but Drew himself. It was like Safe Harbour, Brodie thought. It had personality.

The woman at the reception desk was well-dressed in a muted plaid, and her black hair was upswept. She put

down the telephone and looked up with a smile.
'Hello, Brodie!' she said. 'You haven't been in all
summer.'

'I've been busy, Sue.'

'I'm sorry that you aren't working here now.'

Brodie shrugged. 'I was only a messenger girl last
summer.'

The woman shook her head. 'No, you were much
more than that. You were a real help, and I miss you.'

'Well, that's always pleasant to hear. Is Drew busy?'

'He took the afternoon off.' She sounded a little
surprised that Brodie hadn't known.

Brodie smiled, and a dimple peeked out. 'The golf
course must have cast out an irresistible lure.'

'No. He said he was going home. He hasn't looked
well, lately, Brodie.'

Drew not well? But he was never sick. She couldn't
remember a time when illness had kept him away from
work.

'He looks awfully tired, too,' Sue said, watching
Brodie carefully, 'and as if his mind really isn't on
business.'

Brodie said slowly, 'It isn't anything serious, is it,
Sue?' He'd been just the same as always, she was
thinking, and then realised that in the last week he had
been just a little quieter, and moodier, than she had
ever known him to be. Was he worried about the state
of his health? And if so—It would have to be serious, to
cause Drew to brood.

The woman made a helpless gesture. 'I was hoping
you'd know. Perhaps he should see a doctor,' she
suggested.

Daniel came out of his office and put a legal
document, in its pale blue folder, on the secretary's
desk. 'Who should see a doctor, Sue?'

It was Brodie who answered. 'Drew. He isn't really
ill, is he, Daniel?'

Daniel snorted. 'Of course not. Drew doesn't need a

doctor. Nothing ails him that you couldn't cure, Brodie.'

'Me? What could I do?'

He turned in the doorway of his office and looked her over appraisingly. 'You could stay home and act responsible, for starters,' he said. 'Quit dragging him down to that seedy bar every night.'

'I don't force him to go there!' Brodie retorted.

Daniel looked irritated. 'What is he supposed to do, Brodie? Sit at home and worry about whether you'll make it back safely? That would be just as hard on him.'

'I don't need protection.' But she knew, even as she said it, that it was far from true. As long as Drew was there at the nightclub she felt secure. She had protested the first night, when he had sat through the whole show, that he didn't need to stay and be bored. But she had been grateful to have him there, and he had seemed to read her mind. Every night he stayed through the show, sitting quietly off in a corner, sipping a single drink. She had wondered, sometimes, what he thought about as he waited.

Daniel snorted again. 'That's a joke, Brodie. Just when does Drew have any time for himself? He's here every morning by eight, when you're still sound asleep, I suspect. And he spends all evening and half the night at that . . .'

'It is not a seedy bar,' she said sullenly.

Daniel didn't press it. 'Do you know, for example, how long it's been since Drew played golf?'

She hadn't thought about it, but she couldn't remember him mentioning the game all week.

'It's my opinion the man is just worn out, Brodie. Give him a break. Either stay home, or find an alternate bodyguard, but let Drew off the hook.' He didn't wait for an answer, and the office door shut behind him with a thump.

'I guess I got told,' Brodie said.

'I wouldn't pay any attention to Mr Baxter,' Sue said, but it was weak.

Brodie looked down at her. 'You think he's right, don't you?'

'Well——' Sue hesitated, and then said, 'Mr Hammond does look awfully tired sometimes. And he's never been snappy before, but in the last ten days——'

Ever since he has been watching over me at the club, Brodie thought. 'I can take the hint,' she said drily. 'I'll see you later, Sue.'

'I'm sorry if it hurt.'

'Don't be sorry that you told me what I needed to hear.' Brodie let the door close behind her and took a deep breath of the hot summer air. After the pleasant coolness of the air-conditioned office, the outside air felt like an oven. And it was a long, steep hill up to Safe Harbour.

'The truth is, Bro,' she told herself wryly, 'that you had no interest in Drew's wishes for dinner. You just hoped he'd give you a ride home!'

Safe Harbour was cool and quiet, its thick brick walls holding out the hot sunshine, and she sighed in relief as she let herself in the front door. The library was empty, without even a briefcase on the desk. The drawing room was silent and perfectly neat. Sometimes, Brodie thought, she wanted to walk through that room and give the furniture a push, just to make the place look lived in!

Perhaps, she thought, Drew had gone out to the golf course anyway. She fixed herself a glass of lemonade and went up to her room. Then the murmur of the television from the sitting room drew her down the hall.

He was stretched out in his recliner, sound sleep. The glass of iced-tea on the table beside him had warmed to room temperature. The television babbled on unheeded.

He looked exhausted, his eyes tightly closed as if to hold out anything that might disturb him, two lines cutting deep in his forehead. Even when he's asleep, he's worried, Brodie thought.

Sunlight was pouring in through the windows, and he put a hand up as if to block it out of his eyes. Brodie silently closed the curtains and then curled up in a chair across the dim room, sipping her lemonade, thinking about her future, and watching him sleep.

Was he simply exhausted? Several times it had been well past midnight by the time they left the nightclub, but Drew had never uttered a word of complaint. She hadn't given it a thought. Now, guiltily, she realised how correct Daniel was. Drew had always left the house by the time she stumbled downstairs for her first cup of coffee. Despite her good intentions, she couldn't seem to rise early enough to beat him to the kitchen.

Or was Sue right? If he is ill, Brodie thought. I don't know what I'll do. Visions of one dread disease after another fluttered through her mind, until she told herself crossly to stop imagining ghosts. If there was something wrong with Drew's health, she'd face it when she knew it. That would be plenty of time.

It was almost two hours later that he stirred, blinked, and sat up abruptly, shaking his head to clear it. The sun had passed on to the west, and the room was dim. 'I didn't mean to sleep so long,' he said, seeing her there. 'It's almost dark, so it must be late.'

'Not really. It's not quite seven.' She pulled the curtains back, and light streamed into the room.

'That's a relief. I can take a minute to wake up.' He settled back into his chair with a smile. 'You're not dressed for the club.'

'No.' She uncurled from her chair and walked across the room to turn the television off. 'I need to renegotiate my room rent, Drew. I no longer have an income.'

'Oh?' His voice indicated nothing but mild interest. 'What happened?'

'I quit this afternoon.' Then, reluctantly aware that

she hadn't quite told the truth, she shook her head. 'Actually, I got fired. The manager said I wasn't earning my way.'

Drew was silent for a few minutes. Then his smile flashed. 'Don't worry, Bro. I'll give you a week or two before I start eviction proceedings.' He stood up and stretched. 'What's for dinner? I'm starving.'

She clapped a hand over her mouth. 'I forgot to start anything! I was going to ask what you wanted, but you were asleep—and I forgot.'

He laughed. 'Some kitchen maid you are,' he teased, and ruffled her hair with a careless hand. 'Go put on something snappy and I'll take you to the club. The country club, that is—if I never see the inside of that other one again, I won't miss it.'

She caught his hand and held it pressed against her cheek. He looked down at her, a little surprised, and she said, 'Sue thinks you're ill. Is there anything wrong, Drew?'

'Sue should stick to being a secretary,' he said. 'She'd never make it as a nurse. I'm healthy as a horse, Bro.'

She didn't let go of his hand. 'You wouldn't lie to me, would you?'

He looked offended. 'Me? An honest, upstanding citizen, lie? I'm ashamed of you, Brodie McKenzie.'

She wasn't convinced. 'You've told me a hundred times that there is sometimes a difference between legal facts and the real truth. When was the last time you saw a doctor?'

He looked thoughtful. 'I think it was last Wednesday afternoon when I played golf with my regular foursome.'

'Dammit, Drew, that doesn't count.' She pulled herself up to her full height and stared up at him.

He just laughed at her. 'Go get dressed, Bro. We'll talk about it over dinner.'

The jumbo shrimp were huge, juicy and succulent, and

Brodie was far more interested in them than in arguing with Drew. By the time her plate was empty she was ready to go on the attack again.

But Drew skillfully kept the conversation away from anything that hinted of medicine or health, and Brodie finally gave up. After all, she told herself, he was a grown man, and nobody could force him to do anything he didn't want to.

'What are your plans now?' he asked as she tackled a slice of chocolate cake.

Brodie savoured the taste of coconut frosting and said, indistinctly, 'I don't know. But I'm not going to impose on you at Safe Harbour any longer than necessary. I can't just be a permanent guest there.'

'Why not?'

'Because it isn't fair! As long as it was just a temporary thing, till I got on my feet . . .'

'It's your home, Brodie.'

'Daniel says you might get married. I don't know what kind of a wife would cheerfully accept a grown woman freeloading in her house, but . . .'

'Considering that you don't like Daniel, you certainly pay a lot of attention to what he says,' Drew pointed out.

'Really, Drew. Can you sit there and tell me, honestly, that you've never thought about marrying?'

He swirled the wine in his glass and didn't answer.

'That answers my question,' Brodie said, and scooped up the last crumbs of the chocolate cake.

'The same thing applies to you, Brodie. You might marry.'

She shook her head, definitely.

'Come now. If you're so certain that I've recovered enough from Cynthia that I can consider another woman, what would keep you from finding another man?'

Brodie fumbled for an explanation. 'It's different with me,' she said weakly.

Drew laughed. 'It always is, Bro.'

'No, I mean it. Oh, I'd like to have a home of my own—kids, maybe.' Her voice trailed off as she thought about how barren her life would be without those things she had always considered essential. Two kids, a station wagon and a dog, she told herself wryly, and a husband who played racquetball at the YMCA ... Well, she would be living proof that a woman could do quite well without any of them.

'It looks impossible now, but you'll find as the months pass ...'

'It's been years for you, Drew. And you said yourself that you can never forget your first love.'

He looked at her a little strangely. 'Did I say that? Oh, yes, perhaps I did. Of course that person always remains in the back of your memory. But——'

'That wasn't what you meant, Drew.'

He didn't press the subject. 'You could always go back to school.'

She took her head definitely. 'That's the only thing I'm certain of. I'm finished with college!'

'Or perhaps you want to try another city. If you'd like to try your luck in New York, I'd be glad to help you.'

'No. Thanks, but you'd be throwing good money after bad. The one thing I learned from this experience is that I don't have enough stamina to make a success of it. There's considerable doubt about whether my voice is good enough, too, but I just can't keep going. I'd give up with the first audition refusal.'

'It takes both talent and determination, Bro.' His voice was carefully neutral. 'So what comes next?'

'Well,' she said firmly, 'I need something to do. I thought about going to stay with Janet, and asking her to help me find a job. But I think I'd rather stay at Safe Harbour. Can I have my job back at the law office? Do you need a messenger girl year round?'

'If you want, Bro. But—not using your voice at all.
Can you stand that?'

She pushed the cake crumbs around on her plate.
'Are you upset that I've wasted all that money on
lessons?'

'It wasn't wasted. You may have given up the
stardust world for reality, but I'm confident you'll still
use your training somewhere.'

She shrugged. 'I'll sing in the church choir and
volunteer to do "Oh Promise Me" at weddings. Maybe
I'll give lessons. It was a pipe dream to think I could
make a living at it. Hi, Daniel.' Her voice had a
noticeable lack of enthusiasm as Daniel laid a hand on
her shoulder, bare under the halter neckline of the new
coffee-coloured dress.

'I thought I was hallucinating for a minute when I
first saw you, Brodie,' Daniel went on. 'You aren't
singing tonight?'

'I'm no longer employed there,' she said briefly.

There was a twinkle in his eyes, and the pressure of
his hand increased on her shoulder till Brodie thought
she would be pushed right out of her chair. 'Good girl!'
he said. 'I knew you'd see the light!'

She didn't bother to correct him. What difference did
it make, after all? The sooner the whole episode was
forgotten, the better it would be for Brodie.

He turned to Drew. 'You're looking much better this
evening.'

'A nap does wonders,' Drew said briefly.

'It certainly seems to. I'll see you first thing in the
morning, Drew. I need some time with you, by the
way—we have business to discuss.' He winked broadly
and moved on towards the door with a final squeeze of
Brodie's shoulder.

She rubbed the protesting muscle at the top of her
arm. 'I'm glad Daniel approves of me,' she said tartly,
'but I wish he'd just tell me about it instead of mauling
me!'

'Daniel is such a grizzly bear of a man that he doesn't realise his own strength.'

The waitress refilled Brodie's coffee cup and she thoughtfully stirred the dark liquid. 'Drew—what ever happened to Cynthia, anyway?' she asked curiously, and then held her breath. He'd brought up the woman's name himself a few minutes ago, for the first time ever. Would he answer this question?

He shrugged. 'She got married. Had a son.'

'Do you ever hear from her?'

'From Cynthia? Of course not. About Cynthia? Frequently. She's Daniel's niece, you know.'

'Oh. No wonder I disliked her at sight.'

It was his turn to be curious. 'Do you remember her? You were very young.'

'Vaguely. I just knew that she was a phoney.' Then she bit her lip. 'Sorry, Drew.'

'Out of the mouths of babes . . .' he murmured.

The door to the small patio party room opened and what seemed a hundred people spilled out. Most of them were laughing and excited, some holding champagne glasses high. Among them, Brodie saw, was Jerry. Just what was Jerry doing here, she asked herself. It was hardly the environment he was used to. Then she saw Isabel beside him.

Will I ever reach the point where seeing him doesn't twist my heart into a knot, she wondered. If I could see a crowd of people, and not instantly look for Jerry— just that much would make it easier.

Oliver Fanning had a bottle of champagne in his hand, and he was going from table to table in the restaurant splashing it into glasses. He seized Brodie's glass, brimmed it with the bubbly wine, and filled Drew's as he said, 'Everybody's in on the celebration tonight. The drinks are on me!'

'What's the occasion, Oliver?' Drew asked.

Oliver filled his own glass and took a long drink. 'My girl's engagement party,' he said. 'My little Isabel is getting married!' He held his glass up in a toast and then moved on to the next table.

Brodie's eyes went instantly to the happy bride-to-be, standing with her hand possessively on Jerry's arm. As Brodie watched, the girl reached up to pat his cheek. On her left hand gleamed an enormous diamond.

Brodie's knuckles clenched on the edge of the table, and she stared down at her hand, fighting for control. So Jerry had achieved what he had wanted. All it had taken was the substitution of another girl. Somebody should warn Isabel, she thought drearily.

Drew was watching her over the rim of his cup. Like Brodie, he had left his champagne glass untouched. She looked up at him with shock-bright eyes, and he reached for her hand. 'Perhaps going away for a while would help,' he suggested softly. 'We could rent a cottage down at the lake——'

She shook her head firmly. 'No, Drew. I have to face it here. Running away will only make it harder.' She pleated her napkin with nervous fingers. 'Perhaps it was only me, Drew. Maybe Isabel can make it work.'

There was doubt in his eyes, but he didn't comment. It was a good thing, too, Brodie thought shakily, or she'd have burst into tears. 'Take me home, Drew,' she begged softly.

He pushed his chair back. 'Of course.'

In the cloakroom, Brodie hunted through a hundred silky shawls in search of the tiny cape that matched her dress. She was paying no attention to anything else in her hurry to get out of the club. Once she had found it, she draped it carelessly over her arm.

Drew's fingers closed on her elbow, and he said quietly, 'Wait a minute, Bro.'

'But——' she started to protest, looking up in surprise.

It was only then that she heard the voices in the entranceway.

'Did you see that dress she was wearing tonight? It

certainly left nothing to the imagination.' Brodie
thought she recognised the voice; she'd seen Caroline
Percy in the dining room. And Mrs Percy had looked at
her with one eyebrow raised, as if to say that she had
never been fooled by the lame explanation Brodie had
tried to pass off that night at Safe Harbour.

'Especially his imagination,' Mrs Percy went on. 'She
won't leave him alone.'

'Or is it that he won't let her go?' This voice was a
little softer. 'She moved out once, you know, and he
went right down and brought her back to Safe
Harbour.'

Brodie's eyes widened with horror. She looked up
at Drew. He didn't look shocked, just concerned for
how she would feel at overhearing herself discussed
like that.

'Well, whichever it is, I'm amazed at Drew
Hammond. It's indecent how they're living together and
pretending there's nothing to it all but guardianship.'

'He is her guardian,' the other woman protested
quietly.

'You believe that's all it is?' Caroline Percy laughed
sharply.

'You did say she was engaged when she came home.'

'And so she was. Don't be so innocent, dear. Surely
you can see . . .' The voices trailed off as the woman left
the club.

It was a full minute later before Drew released her
elbow. 'Let's go, Brodie.'

She stood there as if rooted. 'That was horrible.'

'Those who eavesdrop never hear anything good
about themselves. We will talk about it at home, not
here.' His voice was like steel.

It was impossible to argue with him when he sounded
like that. But in the silence of the Lincoln, she said,
'You weren't surprised to hear all that garbage, were
you? You were angry, but not shocked.'

'No, Brodie, I wasn't surprised.'

'How long has it been going on?' The calm, level tone of her voice surprised her.

For a moment, she didn't think he was going to answer. Then he said, very quietly, 'Several years. Since you stopped being a child and became a young woman.'

'They think we're sleeping together.'

'Yes.'

She was suddenly, blazingly angry. 'Why haven't you stopped them? Why haven't you told them the truth?'

He sighed. 'Bro, everybody who knows you or me knows the truth. Those old cats wouldn't believe it if St Joan of Arc herself told them they were wrong.'

'But your reputation—a lawyer's reputation is his fortune, Drew.'

'I haven't noticed business falling off any,' he said drily.

'They can't just make these accusations against you. Why don't you sue them?'

'What would that accomplish? Bringing it all out in court would only publish it through the whole county. It would make everyone think it must be true if I was so upset about it. I hoped that it would go away—that you would never need to know about it.'

She was silent for a long time, huddled in the corner of her seat. 'It's just one more sacrifice you've made for me, is that it, Drew?' The words were bitter.

He parked the Lincoln in the garage and turned towards her, putting an arm across the back of the seat. 'Bro—I don't regret a single thing I've ever done for you. Please believe that.'

'And now I'm asking for one more thing—one last thing. Loan me some money, Drew,' she begged. 'Enough so I can get a new start, somewhere else. I'll go stay with Janet.'

'You said you didn't want to do that.'

'But I have to, don't you see? It's time I did something for you. I'll pay the money back as soon as I'm able, I promise. Then you'll be free of me.'

'A few minutes ago you told me you had to face up to your problems here.'

'That was before I knew I was hurting you!'

'Damn it, Brodie, you aren't hurting me. And neither are those old hens. If they weren't gossiping about us, they''d have chosen someone else.' He slammed the car door and strode across the concrete to the back door.

Brodie followed, looking up at the solid walls, the heavy timbers, the brown brick of Safe Harbour. It's my anchor in a crazy world, she thought.

Always when she had left the house, it was with the comforting feeling that she could come home. Even the last time, the ill-fated try at a career, she had known in the back of her mind that if she didn't make it, Drew would let her come back. But now it was Brodie herself who knew she could never return. Safe Harbour could never be hers again.

She followed Drew down the hall to the library. 'If I pack some clothes, would you take me down to the hotel? Not the one I was at before, though, I won't go there again.'

He slammed a desk drawer. 'Hell, no. I won't take you anywhere because there is no need for you to leave.'

'How can you say that?'

'It's no different today than it was yesterday or last week, Brodie. Because those women think we're living together doesn't change the facts. Stop acting like a child!'

'Then stop treating me like one! I have a right to know what's being said about me!'

He took a deep breath and controlled his voice with an effort. When he spoke again, it was quietly. 'Go into the drawing room and sit down, Brodie. I'll be there in a minute.'

She ignored the comfortable chairs and chose to sit bolt upright on the bench in front of the grand piano. She stared at the elegant furnishings, at the intricate pattern of the Oriental rug, at the oil portrait of Drew's mother that hung above the fireplace. And she didn't see any of them. She saw a long bleak future, without that precious centre that had always been home.

'Brodie?'

He had come in so quietly that she jumped when he spoke. He leaned on the back of a chair and said, 'You told me a little while ago that you wanted to do something for me. I don't think you have to leave here to do that. Will you listen to what I have to say?'

She shrugged and brushed a tear away. 'What do I have to lose?'

He looked at her for a long time, as if unsure of what came next. 'Daniel was right,' he said, finally. 'I have been thinking of getting married.'

Brodie looked down at her hands, clenched so tight together in her lap that her nails were cutting her palms.

'Brodie,' he said softly, 'will you marry me?'

CHAPTER SEVEN

BRODIE felt as if the upholstered piano bench was sliding out from under her. For a moment she thought she hadn't heard right. And then, as she looked up at him, and saw the deadly serious expression in his green eyes, she knew that her ears hadn't suddenly begun to play tricks.

She started to laugh shakily. 'My God, Drew, I thought chivalry died in the Middle Ages! If you're trying to do the honourable thing——'

'You promised you'd listen to what I have to say, Brodie.' His voice was quiet, but firm.

She fell silent, still wondering what on earth had given him such a quixotic notion.

'We've both been hurt by people we cared very much about, Bro. Yours is a fresh wound, and it's hard for you to look ahead. Right now it must feel as if that hurt will never heal. But it will, I assure you it will.'

'You said there's never again a love like the first one,' she reminded.

'That's true. It leaves scars, and once that first love is past——' he hesitated. 'But there are other important things in life, Brodie. There is still affection—and friendship. Perhaps those things are even more lasting, since they don't involve the fires of passion. That all-wonderful thing called being in love burns out sometimes. Affection and friendship don't.'

Marry someone she didn't love? Live—for always—with someone who wasn't Jerry?

'Perhaps a marriage where the friendship comes first might be quieter,' Drew went on, 'but it may also be more lasting. It may not have the fireworks that we've come to expect in a marriage—but it may not have the depths of despair, either.'

He was beginning to make a frightening kind of sense, Brodie thought. Or was it just that her grip on reality was slipping?

'To tell you the truth, that's exactly what I want, Brodie. A comfortable marriage—call it a partnership, perhaps. No emotional storms, no——' He stopped suddenly.

Brodie wondered what kind of temper tantrums Cynthia had treated him to. It must have been difficult for him.

He went on relentlessly. 'You must see, now that Jerry is engaged to Isabel Fanning, how impossible it is that he will ever come back to you, Bro. You cannot have your first love, and that means that you have some choices to make.'

'What choice is there?' she whispered. 'Without Jerry . . .'

'But you can't have Jerry.' He paced the width of the room and turned back to her. 'So you must look at the options that don't include Jerry.'

She shook her head. 'I don't understand.'

'This afternoon you discovered that your plans for a career wouldn't work out. You could be sour and bitter about that—but you chose, instead, to look for a new kind of job, and to sing as a hobby. It's second choice, but right now it's the best that you can manage.'

She shook her head. 'What does singing have to do with it?'

'It's the same thing, Bro. You could choose to be bitter about Jerry, and waste your life mourning because you could not have your first choice. Or you can look around and see what the second choice is.'

She forced a smile. 'It isn't very flattering to you to be second choice, Drew. Don't you want more than that?' She could see the pain in the green depths of his eyes, and she was sorry that she had brought it back to him.

He was silent for a time, as if thinking about it. Then he said, 'I don't want to spend my life alone, Brodie. But it wouldn't be very pleasant, either, to be married to a woman who thought she loved me. If I couldn't love her in return, I don't think it would be worth the emotional turmoil. I want companionship—friendship——'

She reached up to brush his cheek with gentle fingers. 'Cynthia hurt you very badly, didn't she?'

He took a long, unsteady breath. 'We've both been hurt almost beyond bearing, Brodie, by people who didn't love us as much as we loved them. Perhaps we can heal together.'

'And perhaps we will never heal at all,' she said sombrely.

'That may be true. But no pain could be worse than what we've had. Surely we can try to make a new pattern in our lives?'

'Why me, Drew?' she asked suddenly. 'Is all this just an excuse? Because you feel responsible for me?'

'I do feel that way,' he admitted quietly. 'I care about your well-being. I always will, because you're important to me, Bro. But I could satisfy that in a hundred different ways.'

'Then why choose this way?'

'Because you understand the pain, Bro. No other woman knows me so well.' He touched a glossy curl with a gentle fingertip. 'Together we can have security—affection—fondness. We've been friends. All I'm really suggesting is that we put that friendship on a basis that society will accept.'

'Friendship,' she said quietly. 'Is that all you're asking for, Drew?'

'For now,' he said. 'I know that right now the idea of an intimate relationship with anyone but Jerry bothers you ...'

'That's an understatement,' Brodie murmured.

'But with time, you may find as I did that passion may not be the most important part of marriage. And you did say tonight that someday you might want children,' he reminded.

Children—that weren't Jerry's? She shivered. 'I don't know, Drew,' she said, very softly. Then, hesitantly, 'Would you want children?'

There was a long silence. 'I've had much more time than you to consider it, Bro, and I think that I would regret never having a child.'

Colour stained her cheeks. 'I can't promise . . .'

'I'm not asking for promises, Brodie. But it wouldn't be fair not to tell you that I hope that someday we would have children.'

'I haven't agreed to this crazy scheme,' she reminded. 'Much less——' She stared at the carpet, embarrassed by the mere thought. I would feel as if I was cheating Jerry, she thought.

'Nothing comes with a guarantee,' he said gently. 'I'm asking for no promises. I know you can't be sure now how you'll feel in a year or two. But this much I can pledge to you—I will not hurry you, or press you. Until the time comes that you choose differently, Bro, we will go on as we are now, as friends. The only difference will be that piece of paper that makes it legal.'

'What if——' her voice broke, 'what if I never change my mind?'

He smiled, very gently. 'Then we will still be friends, I can promise you that, Brodie.'

She was quiet for a long time and then she asked wistfully, 'Will that be enough for us, Drew?'

He shrugged. 'It's more than either of us will have alone, I've been a very lonely man——' He stopped abruptly and then reached for her hand. It lay cold inside the warm strength of his. 'Bro, if you find a man you care about, the one who can make you forget Jerry and find that breathless love again——'

'He doesn't exist.'

'Then I'll let you go. No questions, no arguments.'

He flicked a gentle finger under her chin. 'What about it, Brodie? Shall we reach out for the comfort we might find together—or shall we walk through life in tight little knots, waiting around in case the supreme happiness wants to seek us out?'

Safe Harbour was almost dark, but Brodie could walk through the rooms unhesitatingly, for she knew every obstacle, every piece of furniture, by heart. She stood by the gothic window that overlooked the tiny second-floor terrace and stared out at the formal gardens. The neat, precise geometrical pathways were a mocking contrast to her whirling thoughts.

'Why can't life be so neatly arranged?' she asked, and let herself drift off for a moment into the perfect world of her imagination where lack of money was never an obstacle to love. Then she pulled herself back with a sharp rein. It needn't have been an obstacle to her romance, either, except that Jerry had determined to marry a wealthy woman. 'And don't forget it again,' Brodie lectured herself.

Moonlight poured down over the garden, and leaves rustled in the soft breeze. The oak trees cast huge shadows that in another season would have been eerie. But tonight there was only the moon, the soft summer wind, and Brodie mulling over her thoughts. The rest of the world was asleep.

She had asked for time to think, and Drew had not pressed for an immediate answer. He had ruffled her hair as he said goodnight, as he had hundreds of times over the years, and now he was peacefully asleep in the big bedroom down the hall.

It didn't seem fair, that he slept while she paced the floor. But Drew never lay awake to entertain doubts and fears, even when the deliberations of a jury hung over his head. Once he had presented his case to the best of his ability, he wasted no time in afterthoughts. Brodie supposed that was how he looked at this proposal, too—as if it were a closing argument and she a jury to be convinced. There certainly was little sentiment involved, as far as Drew was concerned. He saw a need and a way to fill it. Cool, logical, and perfectly sensible. That was Drew.

Well, if she did agree to marry him, she certainly knew what she was getting into, Brodie told herself, and then shook her head in disbelief. She actually sounded as if she was taking this thing seriously, she admitted with a rueful smile.

He was right about one thing, however. She had to begin looking at what she could do with her life without Jerry. Seeing him with Isabel at the nightclub had been a shock, but the announcement tonight of his engagement had felt like a rock-hard fist striking her solar plexus. Until that instant, she had been half-convinced that someday he would realise their love was more important than money. Now Jerry was lost to her forever, in the same stunning day that had taken away her hopes to be a singer and she would have to find a new plan for her life.

What could she do? Brodie nibbled a well-manicured fingernail and assessed her qualifications. Her job skills were few. In several summers of work at the law firm she had collected an amazing command of legal trivia, but one couldn't make a career as a messenger girl. She had worked at no other jobs. Her college classes had been aimed at the single goal of making her a professional singer; anything that didn't—in Brodie's view—lead to that end had received minimal attention. She was trained for nothing.

That was a problem, but it was a manageable one, she decided. The mediocre grades she had brought home had indicated a lack of interest, not a shortage of ability. Much as she despised formal education, she could go back to school next fall and study anything she wanted. If, she reminded herself, Drew was still willing to pay her tuition.

So the important question really was, what did she want to do?

The answer came as a negative, and it startled her. 'I don't want to leave Safe Harbour,' she murmured, voicing aloud the thought that had come so clearly to her mind.

That's silly, she told herself. She had always known that someday she'd go out on her own. Was she only a baby bird, unwilling to leave the nest?

I can't stay here, she told herself. It isn't fair to Drew, to depend on him so. He's already done so much for me, and I can't ask for more.

'But I didn't ask. He asked me to do this for him,' she said. The moonlight seemed to glow a little brighter, as if approving.

What was it Mrs Riley had said, that first day she had come home? It was something about the house being as lonely as its owner. Drew had given up so fearfully much over the years because of Brodie; this was the only thing he had ever asked in return.

It wasn't much. All he wanted was for her to stay at Safe Harbour as she had been doing. The legal formality would satisfy society, but it would make no difference to them.

Why shouldn't she do as he asked? There would be no Jerry in her life, and no one could ever take his place. Perhaps Drew was right. Perhaps together they could find some semblance of happiness.

I do not want to spend my life alone, she thought, any more than Drew does.

She wandered into the guest bedroom that opened on to the little terrace. Moonlight peeked through the loose-woven drapes and played hide-and-seek with the tiny flowers in the wallpaper.

I'll paint it white, she thought absently, and I'll put new paper on one wall. Green and yellow stripes, perhaps. Or circus animals. Something bright, for a baby's eyes to catch and focus on . . .

Suddenly aware of the direction of her thoughts, Brodie clapped her palms to her hot cheeks. Then, deliberately, she forced herself to think about Drew. Could she live with him, sleep with him, bear his children—and love another man?

No, she thought. No. I cannot do that.

But he hadn't asked that of her. All he had asked was for her to keep an open mind about the future. Perhaps he, too, would need time to get used to a wife who wasn't Cynthia.

Brodie had never thought about Drew as a man, just as the pseudo-uncle he had always been to her. Her friend Janet had thought him handsome, and Brodie supposed that Janet was right. Far more important to Brodie was his generosity, his kindness. Those things would not change. They were friends; they would be companions. That was all, unless someday in the dim future——

Her mind still spinning, she finally tumbled into bed, only to dream of Jerry. She was walking down the church aisle to meet him, the heavy white satin of her gown dragging her back, Drew's arm supporting her. As she reached the altar rail Jerry stepped forward to meet her, but instead of taking her hand he folded his arms across his chest and said sternly, 'Where's the money, Brodie? Let's count the money first, and then we'll have the wedding.' When she shook her head, uncomprehending, his face changed and twisted, and his mouth opened in a snarl, and Brodie started to scream.

She found herself moments later clutching the sleeve of Drew's battered old green bathrobe, her face buried in his shoulder as he murmured soothing words into her ear. Finally she sniffed weakly and relaxed, not wanting to lift her head from the comfortable hollow where his heart beat strongly under her ear.

I must get him a new bathrobe for his birthday, she was thinking vaguely.

'Do you want to tell me about it?' he asked.

Brodie shook her head. 'It's past now. Thanks for coming in.'

His voice was gruff. 'I will always come when you call, Bro. Always.'

The morning sun was pouring across her bed when she woke. Brodie stretched lazily and then memory of the night before flooded over her. 'I must give him an answer,' she thought, and stumbled out of bed.

But the house was empty. When she checked his bedroom, the bed was already neatly made and not so much as a dirty sock was evidence that he even occupied the big room.

The downstairs rooms were just as silent, and she left a note for Mrs Riley and started down the hill towards the law office, her heels tapping on the pavement. And ringing in her head with the same rhythm as her footsteps was the question, 'What am I going to tell Drew?'

He was leaning over Sue's desk when Brodie came in, pointing out a paragraph in a contract she was working on. He looked up with a smile, but Brodie could see strain around his eyes. 'It's only nine in the morning and you're wearing shoes?' he asked lightly. 'You must have a big day planned.'

'I came to work,' she said briefly. 'You did tell me last night that I could have my job back.'

'Hallelujah,' Sue said.

'Don't get impatient, Sue,' Drew told her. 'I want to talk to Brodie for a few minutes. Then you can put her to work.'

The solid oak door closed behind them with a refined click, but Brodie felt a little as if it was the steel bars of a jail cell.

'So you want a job,' he said.

Brodie knew the room was soundproof, but she dropped her voice anyway. 'And you want an answer.'

He leaned against the corner of his desk. 'It would be helpful,' he agreed.

Brodie perched on the edge of a chair. 'You weren't joking last night? Trying to cheer me up, or something?'

A smile tugged at the corner of his mouth. 'No. I was serious.'

'Then—yes. With one condition,' she qualified hastily.

His smile seemed to freeze. 'What's the condition, Bro?'

'You said that if it turned out that I was wrong—and I fell in love again—that you'd let me go. The same applies to you. If the right woman comes along, and you want out——'

'That won't happen, Brodie. I don't back out on my promises,' he said gravely.

There was a brief silence. 'I'm scared, Drew,' she whispered.

He put a hand on her chin, and tipped her face up so he could look at her. She was afraid for a moment that he was going to kiss her, that he would expect some sign of passion or love. But he merely brushed her cheek with his lips. 'To tell you the truth, I'm a little scared too,' he admitted. 'It's an unusual thing we're doing——'

' "Crazy" might be a better word for it.'

Drew smiled. 'Shall we go and look at rings this morning?'

Brodie froze. It would be torture to sit down there in the little office at Brooke's Jewellery, and look at the trays of diamonds that she and Jerry had studied so carefully.

'I don't want an engagement ring,' she said, as if the words were being choked out of her. 'Please, Drew, don't make me do that.'

'No ring?' But he didn't sound surprised. 'Very well, Bro. I think we should be married right away.'

'People will talk,' she warned.

'They'll talk more if we give them a few months before the wedding. This way, once the shock is past, there won't be anything to talk about.'

'Very well.' She could work up no enthusiasm for white satin, or orange blossom, or candelabra. Those things were the trappings of love matches. They didn't belong in a marriage of convenience.

'I'll make the arrangements. In the meantime,' Drew continued, 'the fewer people who know . . .'

'I can't think of anyone I want to tell,' Brodie said. There was an edge to her voice. 'Just let me know where to show up.' She rose. 'I think I'd like to go to work now.'

He reached for her hand, and she looked a long way up to meet his eyes. 'Bro——' he said softly, 'thank you. I am honoured.'

'No promises,' she reminded. Her voice was a bare whisper. 'I hope we don't regret this.'

Sue had set her to work at the filing cabinets. 'It seems I never have time to catch up on these things,' she said. 'As soon as I try, something else explodes. We really need another full-time paralegal in this office.' She gave Brodie a warm smile. 'I probably shouldn't tell you all this, or you'll run screaming out the door and never come back!'

'It won't be that easy to get rid of me this time.' Brodie slipped another document back into its proper file. 'What does a paralegal do, anyway?'

'Oh, pretty much what an attorney does. We have to work under supervision, of course, but we can do most of the basic stuff.'

'I thought you were just a secretary.'

'That's how I got started. I could have gone to school, but I decided to work my way up with on-the-job training. As time goes on, there are more things I can handle. Estates, wills, interviewing clients——'

Brodie shrugged. 'All an attorney does is string together standard paragraphs and put in a lot of "whereases" and "heretofores" and call it a legal document.'

'You'd better not let Mr Hammond hear you talking like that,' Sue warned.

'It was Drew who told me. He also said once that law school just taught you which book to look in. But I'm not sure he meant that,' she added thoughtfully, upon reflection.

Sue would have pushed it, but Oliver Fanning came in just then, loud and booming as always and with Isabel trailing like a shadow behind him. 'I need to see Drew,' he announced in a voice that would have rattled Notre-Dame Cathedral.

Sue smiled politely. 'I'll see if he can fit you in, Mr Fanning.'

Isabel wandered over to the filing cabinet where Brodie was assembling a case file in proper order. 'Do you have a new job? It must not be very exciting, after being a singer.'

'Perhaps not, but I meet a nicer class of people,' Brodie returned sweetly.

'I saw you last night at the country club. Sorry I couldn't come over to talk to you, but Jerry was introducing me to some of his friends.'

If Jerry had brought his friends to the club last night, Brodie thought, it had probably turned into a riot by midnight.

'He's my fiancé, you know,' Isabel added ingenuously.

'I gathered that last night.'

'That's what we came in for this morning. Daddy wants to talk to Mr Hammond about the prenuptual agreements. He wants to get everything straightened out right away.'

Drew opened his office door, and Oliver Fanning said, 'You just wait out here, Isabel. This won't take long.'

At least he's doing something to protect her from Jerry, Brodie thought. But if it was my fiancé they were discussing, I'd be right in there listening.

Isabel, however, didn't seem to mind being left out of the discussion.

'When is the wedding?' Brodie asked. She didn't really care, but it was the only polite thing to do.

'In three weeks. Daddy's giving us a trip to Jamaica for a wedding gift.' Isabel's eyes were bright.

'You're going to the Caribbean in July?' Instantly Brodie regretted the tactless question. Then she reflected, at least I didn't say anything about what a hurry she's in.

Isabel's jaw tightened. 'I've always wanted a honeymoon in the Caribbean, and I don't see why I shouldn't have it, no matter when the wedding is.'

'Well, it's your wedding.' Brodie's tone was placating.

'My dress is being custom-made. And——' Isabel prattled on for several minutes.

Brodie thought she understood. To most people, the girl's shyness made her a crashing bore, but she had suddenly found herself the centre of attention. Even her father was abruptly forced to notice her. And Isabel was determined to enjoy the glow.

The pile of documents started to slide off the edge of the table, and both girls grabbed for them. Isabel's sleeve slipped, and as Brodie looked up to thank her for the help, she saw a shadow on Isabel's arm, right above the elbow. It almost looked like the mark of fingerprints.

Isabel saw her glance at the mark and quickly pulled the sleeve back into place.

It's none of my business, Brodie told herself uneasily. I don't know that Jerry made those marks. I couldn't even swear that it was a bruise. For all I know, maybe the girl just skipped her bath last night. But——

'Isabel,' she said, very softly, 'be careful. Don't let yourself be hurt.'

Isabel laughed, a tinkling little sound. 'What do you mean, Brodie? Who would want to hurt me? You've never been in love, have you? You can't understand what it's like, then, to have someone be so desperately in love with you that he would do anything for you.'

'That's right,' Brodie murmured. 'I've never been quite that lucky.'

'You sound jealous, Brodie.' Isabel preened a little. 'We never did have tea together. I would still like your advice on redecorating Daddy's house—Jerry and I will be living there after the wedding. Would you like to come next week?'

'I'll have to let you know, Isabel.' Brodie kept her voice even with an effort. There was nothing she wanted less than to become chummy with Isabel now, but she had little choice. The girl's father was a valuable client, and Brodie was now an employee of the firm.

Oliver Fanning reappeared in the door of Drew's office, his voice booming. 'We'll see you next week then for the signing, Drew—Jerry and Isabel and I. Come along, Isabel. Stop bothering the girls.'

She followed him out the door. In that instant, her attitude had changed back to the shrinking violet who cowered away from any hint of disapproval.

'Well!' Sue said with a sigh of relief when the door had closed. 'Talk about Lady Bountiful! If she'd been here another two minutes, I'll bet she'd have offered to fix you up with a blind date.'

Isabel was another one to whom the news of Brodie's marriage would come as a shock, she thought. And Jerry? Just what would Jerry think?

CHAPTER EIGHT

THE stone church was cool this morning, despite the June heat outside and the worshippers who crowded the seats. Brodie tried desperately to keep her mind on the service, but her thoughts kept skipping back to the simple ceremony in the little chapel just a few minutes before, the brief words that had made her Drew's wife.

I am actually married, she kept repeating over and over to herself. Those few words, a promise to love, honour, and cherish, and I'm no longer Brodie McKenzie, but Brodie Hammond.

I certainly don't feel married, she thought, looking down at the gleam of intricately carved gold on her left hand. Drew had not argued the matter of an engagement ring, and so the wide gold band on her finger was alone. He had chosen it, as he had made all the arrangements without consulting her. She had not complained. Once upon a time she had dreamed of the wedding she wanted, but it would have been disloyal to Jerry if she had pursued those plans with another man.

Of course, she told herself, Drew had wanted no complications, either. Just simplicity, and elegance—the things that were expected of a Hammond. The matter of the engagement ring was a good example, Brodie thought. She raised a slim hand to toy with the trinket that gleamed against the creamy skin of her throat. She hadn't told him that she would not wear a diamond; she had merely said that she didn't want a ring. And so this morning he had handed her a full-carat solitaire diamond on a gold chain. The stone had flashed fire in her hand.

'Drew, you could cool off a glass of tea with an ice cube this big,' she had accused.

'That's a thought,' he'd agreed cheerfully, and fastened the chain around the throat before she could argue.

Now, Brodie's fingertip caressed the slick surface of the stone. She stole a sideways look at Drew, under the brim of her straw hat, as if expecting that a stranger would be sitting next to her. He seemed to be concentrating on the pastor's words, and so she studied him covertly for a few moments, almost as if she had never seen him before.

Love, honour, and cherish, she thought. Well, honour would present no problem. She had a very deep respect for Drew, as a man, as an attorney, as a person. She would honour him, and cause no embarrassment to the Hammond name. And cherish—she could certainly do that. In that brief wedding ceremony, the pastor had talked about cherishing, and said that the word meant to hold dear, to be affectionate, to nurture. Yes, Brodie thought, she could do that. All that she needed to do was to follow Drew's example, for had he not cherished her throughout the years?

That left love. Two out of three isn't bad, she told herself wryly.

The choir began to sing, and Brodie noted with detached interest that there was plenty of room for another strong voice in that group. She made a mental note to talk to the director after the services, and wondered if she could convince Drew to join her. His lovely baritone would be a natural addition to the blend of voices.

'I'd like to take a moment before our service ends to welcome our visitors,' the pastor said. 'And to introduce two people who are certainly not new to this church, but who have a new status in our community—Mr and Mrs Drew Hammond, who were married this morning in our chapel.' His smile was that of a mischievous saint.

Heads turned all over the church. Brodie could feel

the astonishment that swept through the congregation like a tidal wave. Caroline Percy was sitting two rows ahead of them, and her head whipped around so fast that Brodie thought the woman's neck might actually snap. Then the surprise in Mrs Percy's face was replaced by a calculated stare, and Brodie's heart sank. What if, instead of stopping the gossip, this hasty marriage only fuelled it? What if Drew's assessment had been wrong?

The service came to a mercifully quick close, and then they were surrounded in the centre aisle by a chattering crowd. Brodie was speechless. She had known, of course, that there would be comment, but if she had realised the extent of the surprise she might have backed out altogether. But Drew, his arm possessively around her waist, accepted the congratulations, intercepted the questions, sidetracked the speculation with a disarming smile, and all the time kept guiding Brodie imperceptibly towards the exit.

Isabel planted herself in their path. 'Well! If you aren't a dark horse, Brodie,' she exclaimed. 'All that talk last week about my wedding, and never a breath about yours. Shame on you, my girl! I'd like you to meet my fiancé, Jerry Whitcomb. Jerry, this is——'

'Brodie,' he said, and the word dripped accusation. His eyes were almost black with anger. Or was it hurt, Brodie wondered, and decided that in any case it didn't matter. Then he looked up at Drew. 'Hammond, I've half a mind to——'

'Offer us your congratulations?' Drew asked pleasantly, and his arm tightened around Brodie, pulling her down the aisle to the main door, away from Jerry's accusing eyes.

Her throat was tight with tears. If I could only talk to Jerry, she thought, explain it to him ...

The pastor was waiting at the door, his hand outstretched. 'I know I've seen you somewhere before,' he told Drew with a grin. 'Your face certainly rings a bell.'

'I hope you're proud of yourself,' Drew retorted. 'The stampede almost trampled my wife.'

'And a lovely bride she is, too,' the pastor said, kissing Brodie's hand with a flourish. 'Sorry about the mob, Drew. But I can never resist creating a scene. I would have made a great movie director, don't you think?' he added meditatively.

Brodie saw Daniel waiting for them on the church steps, and instinctively she braced herself for his bear hug. But he didn't touch her, and she was vaguely surprised at the coolness in his voice. After a moment's thought, though, she supposed she should have anticipated that reaction. As Daniel saw it, Brodie would now be even more of a burden to Drew.

Then Drew's hand tightened on her arm, and he said quietly, 'Hello, Cynthia.'

Brodie hadn't seen the blonde at Daniel's elbow until then. She had to look up a couple of inches to meet Cynthia's eyes, which were as hard and purple as amethyst.

Ten years had not been kind to Cynthia Tandy. If her hair didn't owe its blonde gleam to chemicals, Brodie thought, she'd eat it. And the brilliant sunlight revealed tiny wrinkles in the heavily-tanned face that Brodie had remembered as flawless.

Cynthia didn't waste much time watching Brodie. She turned her attention back to Drew, and batted her eyelashes up at him. 'It's so nice to see you again,' she breathed in a husky whisper.

'Will you be staying long?' Drew asked. Brodie thought he sounded just a little breathless, as if keeping his voice level was an effort. Her heart went out to him. To come suddenly face to face with the woman who had been in his heart all these years—the pain must be agonising. Was Drew seeing Cynthia as she really was, Brodie wondered, or as the lovely girl she had been?

'A few weeks at least. I wanted Eric to get to know

Uncle Daniel better. You knew I have a little boy, didn't you, Drew? He's eight, now.'

'Yes,' he said quietly. 'Daniel had told me. You remember Brodie, don't you, Cynthia?'

'How could I forget? She was always underfoot,' the blonde said. 'We really must catch up on old times, Drew. Come to dinner at Daniel's one day this week?' She laid a hand on his lapel and smiled confidently up into his eyes.

Brodie held her breath. Surely he'd turn the invitation down, she thought. But Drew hesitated only a moment before saying, 'Of course we'll come, Cynthia. Name the day.'

Brodie could have hit him. Why drag me into it, if you want to have dinner with your old flame, she wanted to scream. I don't ask you to spend the evening with Jerry. And it was painfully obvious that Cynthia had not intended to include Brodie in their intimate reunion.

But Daniel was Drew's partner; he could scarcely turn down the invitation. For Drew to ignore Cynthia would be just as noticeable as if Brodie were to publicly snub Jerry—the whole town would be talking about it within hours. The gossip would be even worse if Brodie refused to go with him.

And deep in Brodie's tender heart, she understood that it was painful enough for Drew just to see Cynthia again, but to have her become the subject of gossip would be unbearable for him.

You'll just have to go along Brodie, she told herself. It's part of the bargain. Each of us is hurting, and the deal is that we each help to heal the other's pain. Funny, she mused, that she had expected Drew to be there when she needed him, but somehow she hadn't anticipated that he would need her.

Damn Cynthia, she thought bleakly. If she had to show up at all, why did she have to choose today? And damn Daniel, Brodie added to herself. Some partner he was, without even the decency to warn Drew what was coming.

Nobody ever said this was going to be easy, she told herself crossly. She understood that she was taking a gamble. She knew the odds quite well. But throw Cynthia into the deal, and all bets were suddenly off.

Brodie arranged the lump of piecrust on the pastry cloth and cautiously began to roll it out.

'Don't be afraid of it, Mrs Hammond,' Mrs Riley said. There was a twist to her voice, as if she had trouble forming the words.

Brodie looked up with a smile. 'I think we'd both be more comfortable if you just called me Brodie,' she began. 'After all, nothing has really changed around here.'

'That's for sure,' Mrs Riley said. 'I don't know what you're up to, Brodie McKenzie—but it makes me want to spank you.' Then she bit her tongue.

The sudden marriage had come as a tremendous shock to Mrs Riley, Brodie knew. The housekeeper was confused by the fact that Brodie hadn't moved into Drew's big front bedroom and that their actions around Safe Harbour bore no resemblance to those of a pair of lovers.

No wonder that Mrs Riley didn't understand. She'd been walking around looking bewildered all week. But at least most of the time she was keeping quiet about it, Brodie thought. That was some comfort.

The doorbell pealed. 'I'll get it,' Mrs Riley volunteered, and whipped off her apron on her way down the hall.

Brodie's piecrust ripped down the centre, and she looked down at it with a sigh. One instant Mrs Riley was telling her to treat the pastry gently so it didn't get tough and the next, she said, 'Don't be afraid of it.' Brodie couldn't seem to get the hang of it at all.

Mrs Riley came back. 'Isabel Fanning,' she said

briefly. 'She has a package for you. I put her in the drawing room.'

Brodie wiped the flour off her hands. 'Anyone who doesn't call before she comes deserves to see me like this, right?' she asked. Without waiting for an answer, she padded barefoot down the hall to the drawing room.

Isabel was inspecting the oil portrait that hung above the mantel. She turned, unhurried, when Brodie came in. 'I hope I didn't interrupt anything important.'

'I'm just baking a pie.'

Isabel's laugh trilled. 'How domestic! No, really, I'm not laughing at you, Brodie. In fact, I'm looking forward to doing a few things like that myself as soon as I'm married.'

For Jerry, Brodie thought with a pang. His favourite is fudge brownies with marshmallow frosting ... 'Housekeeping does have occasional charms,' she said. 'Won't you sit down, Isabel?'

'I just brought you a little something. I'd have given you a party if I'd known, but since you didn't have the decency to tell anybody you were getting married——'

The box was large and flat, like a dress box, and Brodie opened it with foreboding. But Isabel's taste in lingerie was faultless.

She lifted the white lace négligé out of the box with gentle fingers. 'It's lovely, Isabel.'

'I thought perhaps Drew would like it.' She giggled as Brodie started to blush. 'White seems to be your colour.'

'Well—thank you.' She closed the box and set it aside just as Mrs Riley wheeled in the tea cart.

'What's it like?' Isabel asked, dropping two lumps of sugar into her teacup. 'Being married, I mean.'

Who knows? Brodie thought. This isn't being married, it's playing house.

Isabel didn't seem to notice that there had been no answer. 'I think it will be so much fun,' she said. 'We're going to get a cute little apartment next year and when Jerry's in school I can do all sorts of handy little things. Then after he graduates we'll come back and probably live with Daddy.' She made a face. 'That won't be so nice. I'll have to entertain, then, because of both Jerry and Daddy being executives in the company. But I guess I can learn.'

Brodie sipped her tea and listened to the girl's excited chatter. I must have sounded like Isabel when I first came home, she thought with sudden insight. Amazing, how she had done so much growing up in just a few weeks.

'I just can't imagine being married to someone so much older,' Isabel went on. 'Brodie, Drew must be ten years older than you!'

'Twelve,' Brodie said quietly. I used to feel that way, she thought, remembering how shocked she had been when Janet had admired Drew. Twelve years used to feel like forever.

'That much?' Isabel sounded horrified. 'I suppose in that case he'll want to have babies right away. If he waits much longer, he'll be too old to enjoy them.'

Isabel was making it sound as if Drew was about to collect a pension, Brodie thought with quick resentment. And then she began to feel frightened. Isabel could be right. Drew might not be content to wait very long. And when the day came that he asked her to really become his wife, what if she could not go through with it? Fear rippled through her veins. She hadn't made any promises, but it had been implicit in their agreement that someday it would change. Drew had every right to expect that it would become a normal marriage. What if she couldn't bring herself to agree?

I'll think about it later, she told herself firmly.

'I'm so glad that Jerry isn't anxious to have kids. He wants to establish himself first. Daddy's so proud because Jerry wants to work his way up in the company. He doesn't want Daddy just to give him a job, he wants to earn it. And he insists that he won't take money from Daddy, either. Except for his salary, of course, and living in the house. He says it isn't fair to make me live in a small apartment after I'm used to the big house, and since Daddy only uses a little of it, there's no sense in it going to waste.'

Brodie leaned forward in her chair. 'Isabel——' she said urgently. 'Think hard about it. You don't know Jerry very well. Don't jump into this marriage.'

Isabel drew herself up haughtily. 'I know everything I need to know about Jerry. Because he was born into a poor family doesn't mean that he's inferior.'

It was eerie, like listening to an echo of her own voice trying to convince Drew that Jerry was wonderful. She tried to find words to explain herself, and gave up. Isabel would not listen to anything just now—particularly from Brodie.

'You don't know anything about him,' Isabel added flatly.

'You'd be surprised,' Brodie said.

'Oh, I know that he dated you. Does that surprise you? Jerry told me after we saw you at church yesterday. He said you wanted to get serious, but he wasn't ready yet. He said that until he met me, he didn't know what love really was.' She preened herself just a little.

Brodie was speechless. The devil, she was thinking. What he had said was, strictly speaking the truth—just true enough that if she tried to deny it, she'd end up looking foolish.

'I'm not upset with you, Brodie. I can understand that you found him attractive. After all, Jerry is a wonderful guy.'

Brodie couldn't have said anything if she had tried.

Isabel shrugged and reached for her handbag. 'I hope you and Drew will be very happy.' *And I'm not sorry that you had to settle for second best,* her tone said, under the polite words. 'I'm sure that being married to

Drew will have advantages for you, Brodie. I can't believe the size of that diamond you're wearing.'

Brodie's hand went automatically, protectively, to cup the stone.

'I should think you'd be afraid to wear it all the time like that. It really does look a bit out of place with bare feet.'

Brodie was never quite certain of what she said, but apparently it was bland and polite, for Isabel was smiling when she left. Brodie felt like a thundercloud, and she went back to the kitchen and banged the rolling pin down on the piecrust, wishing that it was Isabel's face there on the countertop.

She was picking strawberries in the garden when Drew came home. He left the Lincoln beside the back door and came up the flagstone steps. 'Need some help?'

'They stain,' she warned absently, and picked a particularly luscious berry. She sat down on the stone wall that surrounded the strawberry bed, and started to nibble at the fruit.

'You're the one who'll get stains,' Drew warned, mopping up a steak of strawberrry juice from her chin. 'No wonder your basket is almost empty—you're eating them as fast as you're picking.'

'Isn't that what berries are for?'

'Leave a few for me,' he ordered. 'Aren't you glad to see me?'

'Sure. Why?'

'You don't look like it. You used to be happy when I came home.'

'Oh. Sorry. Warn me when to expect you tomorrow and I'll have the brass band ready.' She forced a smile. 'Drew would you object if I started giving music lessons? Piano and voice?'

'Why would I object?' He selected the largest berry out of her basket and ate it whole.

'I don't know. It doesn't quite fit with the

atmosphere of Safe Harbour, I guess. But I need something to do.'

'That's a good enough reason.' He looked for another perfect berry. 'Are you tired of the law office already?'

'Of course not. But Sue doesn't need me all the time, and Mrs Riley has everything done around here . . .'

He smiled down at her and then perched on the wall beside her, one arm braced behind her, his eyes narrowed as he surveyed the city spread out in the valley. 'Just start out small so if you don't like it you can quit.'

'I already have one student. Sue's daughter wants to study piano.' Brodie set the basket aside and drew her heels up on the top of the wall, clasping her arms around her knees. 'Must we go to dinner at Daniel's tonight?' she asked plaintively.

He smiled. 'I doubt that Daniel would accept a headache as an excuse, Bro.'

'Daniel is a headache!' she snapped. 'I heard him this morning at the office, telling you what a fool you were to have married me. Just what makes it his business, after all?'

'Daniel thinks my father would have lectured me about it, so he's taken over the job.' Drew sounded very casual about the whole thing.

'Would Andy have thought it was a stupid thing to do?' Brodie's voice was very small.

For a long time, she thought that he hadn't heard her at all. Then he turned to look down at her, the laugh lines at the corners of his eyes crinkling. 'Honey, he'd have been right there cheering.'

The uncertainty in her eyes brought seriousness to his. His arm was a warm bulwark at her back, and Brodie leaned against him with an unconscious sigh. It was so peaceful here, she thought, on this warm hillside just a few yards from Safe Harbour, with the sunshine pouring down and the flowers swaying in the soft breeze, and Drew beside her. She raised her face to his, intending to tell him how wonderful it felt to be back at Safe Harbour.

'Bro,' he said, on a long breath, and then his mouth was warm against hers, not harsh or demanding, but as if he were asking a question.

For a long moment she lay passive in his arms. Then, with a sigh, he released her. 'Sorry,' he said. 'I didn't mean to do that.'

Brodie shrugged. 'It was just an ordinary kiss.'

'Ordinary?' His voice was dangerously quiet.

She turned to look up at him with curiosity, her nerves jangling a warning. But there was no time for an argument or persuasion.

He was in no hurry as he caressed her heavily lashed eyelids, her delicate earlobes, her small, pointed chin. And when he turned his attention to her lips again, it was no commonplace kiss. Brodie felt as if she was paralysed in his arms. She could not pull away from him. His hands were warm through the thin fabric of her cotton shirt. His touch was gentle, and yet there was a tautness about him, as if he was barely controlling himself.

And when he finally released her, she could scarcely keep her balance there on the stone wall. He caressed her chin with the tip of a finger. 'We'll be late to Daniel's,' he warned. 'We'd better hurry.'

'I want to finish picking these berries,' Brodie said unsteadily.

She watched him thoughtfully as he walked towards the house, whistling. It wasn't fair, she fumed. He had been toying with her, teasing her, and then he walked away and told her to hurry so they wouldn't keep Cynthia waiting. The whole truth was that he didn't want to have to explain to Cynthia that he was late because he'd been kissing his wife in the garden. Brodie turned back to the berry patch. Men! she thought. They were all a mystery.

'Touching demonstration of affection. You're quite a pair of lovebirds after all.'

'Jerry!' She looked up in shock. He'd come up the driveway very quietly, on foot. 'You startled me.'

'Did you just expect me to quietly go away? Tell me, Brodie, what's behind this sudden marriage of yours? Did you suddenly discover that you didn't love me after all? Or did you marry Hammond just to get even with me?'

Brodie didn't answer. She hadn't seen him alone since that day in the kitchen when her world had fallen apart; since then, they had always been in a public place, surrounded by other people, when they met. 'I can't see that it's any of your business now, Jerry.'

'It's me you love, Brodie. I'm sure of it. Love doesn't just vanish like that.'

'Yours for me didn't seem to last long,' she commented. Her hands were shaking just a little as she picked the plump berries.

'That's not true. I care about you, Brodie. I always will.' There was no doubting the sincerity in his voice.

My first love, she was thinking. 'The invitation to your wedding came in last week's mail, Jerry. I'd rather not talk about our feelings for each other any more.'

'But you can't deny that we have them.' His tone was almost triumphant.

'I have to go in.'

'Have lunch with me tomorrow,' he suggested.

She turned to stare at him. 'Wouldn't Isabel object?'

'She understands.'

'Sometimes I wonder just how much she does understand,' Brodie mused. She picked up her basket and started towards Safe Harbour. She didn't look back, though she knew that Jerry stood there in the driveway watching her.

She was wearing her coffee-coloured dress, and the

diamond necklace twinkled just above the deep neckline. She half-expected that Drew would have a comment, but he merely looked her over gravely. Daniel, though, displayed a reluctant twinge of approval as he opened the door for them. 'Cynthia's not down yet,' he said.

When you're over thirty, it takes longer to make yourself look eighteen, Brodie thought tattily, and gave Daniel her most charming smile.

'Have a drink in the meantime?' he asked, and ushered them out on to the patio. 'After dinner, we'll have a rematch of that last chess game, Drew. This time I won't let you off so easily.'

'If you insist, Daniel.'

'What's the matter, Drew? Don't want to be separated from your bride?' Daniel's voice was tart. 'Cynthia will take care of her.'

His words smarted. Brodie wished that everyone would stop treating her as if she was four years old and needed a babysitter.

Daniel went to call to Cynthia, and Drew leaned back in his chair, swirled his drink, and said, 'By the way, Bro—next time you talk to Jerry Whitcomb, tell him that if he sets foot on my property again he'll be thrown off it.'

So he had seen Jerry. Had he been watching her, or had it been chance that he had glanced out a window in the few minutes she and Jerry had stood there? In any case, she thought, furious, why bring it up here, and now—when Cynthia might walk into the room at any moment?

Brodie sipped her wine and said sweetly, 'When you refer to your property, Drew, do you mean Safe Harbour? Or me?'

'Either,' he said.

'I believe that document we signed was a marriage licence, not a bill of sale,' she said coolly.

Drew didn't seem to hear. 'If I have to go to court to

keep him out of Safe Harbour, I will,' he said. 'That wouldn't please Oliver Fanning, would it?'

Cynthia came in just then, her blonde hair pulled up in a knot atop her head, her dress a spot of brilliant flame-red in the elegant room. Brodie was watching Drew, however, and she saw the quick intake of breath and the fleeting shadow of pain that crossed his face. Then the moment was past, and he was on his feet, smiling, holding a chair for Cynthia.

Brodie's anger melted away as a wave of sympathy swept over her. She knew that feeling well. Half of him wanted to see Cynthia—looked for her, longed to catch a glimpse of her. But the other half felt the hopelessness and the pain, and wanted to hide away somewhere that the beloved person would never come. It was the same for Brodie when she saw Jerry.

And if it was still this way for Drew, after all these years, she thought, then what chance is there that the hurt will ever heal?

Cynthia accepted the martini Daniel handed her with a grateful sigh. 'To old friends,' she said, raising the glass high, and looking at Drew was enormous, soulful eyes. 'I don't know what I would have done if it hadn't been for Hammond's Point, Drew. Just to be able to come back here, to the peace I remember, rests my soul in this terrible time.'

What terrible time was Cynthia suffering, Brodie wondered. She looked great tonight. The evening light was far more flattering to her than the harsh sunlight outside the church had been. She looked at least five years younger and as if nothing whatever was bothering her.

'Uncle Daniel has invited Eric and me to stay all summer, if we like. The separation has been such a blow to Eric, you know. Not that he and his father were ever close, but now that I've actually filed for divorce——'

Divorce? Brodie's glass was suddenly heavy in her

hand, and she moved very carefully to set it down so that it didn't spill. Cynthia was getting a divorce?

She turned to look at Drew, and watched as he raised his glass, and took a long drink. She thought she saw his hand trembling, but there was no evidence in his face that he had had a shock. Was this the face Drew showed when he played poker, or got a surprise in the middle of a trial? Or had he known?

Brodie's head was whirling. If he had known, that would explain his irritation with her for talking to Jerry. Or would it? It certainly didn't explain that kiss in the garden tonight. Or did it?

Brodie's head was whirling. If Drew's first love will soon be free, she wondered, where does that leave me?

CHAPTER NINE

THE meal seemed to drag out forever. Cynthia, playing hostess, scarcely took her eyes off Drew, who was on her right. Brodie sat silent through most of the meal, listening to their bantering conversation, keeping her eyes on her plate, trying to ignore the heavy-handed humour that Daniel continually added.

Drew seemed to be quite at ease, she thought resentfully. He and Cynthia were having a great time catching up on the intervening years. Had the news that Cynthia was seeking a divorce made so much difference to him, then? In the space of a breath, it seemed, his mood had changed from humourless to happy.

Several times, Brodie knew that Drew was watching her, but she refused to meet those slate-green eyes. She knew too well the look of concern she would see there, and she was too confused just now to put on any kind of convincing front. Too confused, and too afraid to let him see how much the idea of Cynthia's divorce had upset her.

She was searching her memory for clues. It was suddenly urgent that she understood what was happening here. Questions that had not occurred to her before were suddenly screaming inside her head.

Had Drew known that Cynthia was coming? He must have, Brodie thought. Daniel would not have kept such a visit secret; he'd have had no reason not to tell Drew. Try as she might, Brodie could not pretend that Drew had been surprised to meet Cynthia outside the church. He might have been startled to see her on that particular day, but he had not been shocked that she was there. He must have known, by the time he had proposed to Brodie, that Cynthia would soon be back in town.

So if Drew had known that Cynthia was coming, why had he pushed for a quick marriage? Why had he proposed at all? The questions ran in circles inside her head, like a frantic hamster in a cage.

Daniel pushed his chair back. 'Time for chess, Drew. Let's see if you've improved your game since the last time I massacred your entire army.'

Brodie felt resentment rising inside her, and then firmly pushed it down. Drew was a guest in Daniel's house; he could not simply refuse to do as his host asked. She sat quietly, staring into her coffee cup.

'Yes, go have a good game,' Cynthia urged. 'Brodie and I will keep each other company, and we'll all have dessert later. Drew, please forgive the state of Daniel's study. He's been so generous about taking Eric and me in, but after living alone so long, it's hard for him to adjust to having a crowd around. So I've left his study entirely alone.'

How charming of her, Brodie thought, to let the man have a whole room to himself. After all, it was still his house.

But Daniel only smiled. 'It's a nice change to have laughter around. And such a nice surprise that Cynthia will be staying a while. I don't mean that the divorce was pleasant news; nothing of the sort. But I'll certainly benefit.' He grinned down at Brodie. 'She didn't tell me about the divorce, you know, till she got here. She was afraid I'd disapprove. Can you imagine, Brodie, that this little girl was afraid of what I'd think?'

Brodie managed to mumble something polite. Drew must have known his old flame was coming back to town with her son, she thought. He must have assumed, as anyone would, that Cynthia was still married. And Drew, being human, had not wanted Cynthia to know that he still carried that years-old flame for her, so he had proposed to Brodie.

His action made a terrible kind of logical sense; it solved both their problems at a blow. But Brodie wished, deep in her heart, that Drew had been honest with her. If he had only told her that Cynthia was coming back—

She wouldn't have married him. It was as simple as that. And Drew was no fool, so he had said nothing about it.

Well, Brodie told herself angrily, he'd turned out to be pretty foolish after all. Cynthia would soon be free, but now they would have to wait not only for her divorce, but his. All he had accomplished was to confuse things, and to slow down his own reach for happiness.

At least Brodie could spare him the embarrassment of asking to be set free. As soon as we get home tonight, she decided, I'll tell him that he can have his freedom. It wouldn't take long to make it official again, after what must be the shortest marriage in legal history . . .

And she swallowed the anger and bitterness that rose in her throat—if he'd just used a bit of sense, she was thinking, it would have spared both of us a whole lot of trouble!—and turned a pleasant smile on Cynthia.

The woman looked like a cat. She really did, Brodie decided, with slanted eyes and that general air of watchfulness, as if Brodie were a parakeet in a cage. But if that was what Drew wanted . . .

'More coffee?' Cynthia asked politely.

'Yes, please.' She'd already drunk so much that if she slept at all tonight it would be a miracle. What difference could one more cup make?

Cynthia filled her own cup and looked across the table with a speculative gleam in her eyes. 'You're quite the mystery lady, aren't you? Tell me, Brodie, were you serious about this whole thing with your boyfriend, or was it all just a play for Drew's sympathy, so he'd marry you?'

The sudden attack took Brodie by surprise. Her hand jerked and coffee slopped over the rim of the cup and formed a puddle in the saucer. Drew had told Cynthia about her? Had confided in her about Jerry?

'You did a good job,' Cynthia went on. 'Drew is so touched by your broken heart that he would do anything you wanted. He's always felt responsible for you—always thought it was up to him to sacrifice so that you would be happy. And now that you're the lady of the manor, I'm sure you're quite satisfied with yourself. Why should you care if Drew is happy? You've always walked all over him.'

There was just enough truth there that it smarted, and it made Brodie want to fight back. 'Nobody forced him to marry me,' she said softly. 'It was Drew's idea.'

'Which you had carefully planted, I'm sure. But why do you think he did it in such a hurry?' Cynthia sipped her coffee and casually answered her own question. 'Because if he'd waited, there were plenty of people who would have tried to talk him out of it. And Drew knew they were right, so he didn't give them a chance to convince him.'

'If you're so concerned about Drew's happiness,' Brodie said, 'why didn't you marry him years ago?'

'Because I was dumb,' Cynthia said bluntly. 'I couldn't see tying myself down to a dry-as-dust country lawyer, just like Uncle Daniel, in Hammond's Point.'

'And now you've changed your mind?'

'Well, Drew is hardly like Uncle Daniel, is he? I imagine you've found that out by now.'

'Doesn't it bother you?' Brodie asked curiously. 'To set out to deliberately break up a marriage . . .'

Cynthia laughed. 'I wouldn't exactly call your arrangement a marriage. Really, Brodie.'

Brodie fought down a blush. Apparently Cynthia and Drew had left no matters undiscussed.

'I didn't quite tell you the whole truth a bit ago,

Brodie. The main reason I turned Drew down years ago was you. I don't plan to let you get in my way again.'

'I don't understand.'

'You were only a little kid at the time, and I could see what was going to happen. Drew's father had just died, and I wasn't about to become stepmother to a brat. I wanted a husband, not a ready-made family. Drew wouldn't consider handing you over to someone else to raise, so we parted company.'

'Because of me?' Brodie whispered. She was horrified.

'I didn't think he would ever have told you that. Good old self-sacrificing Drew, never even letting anyone know what he's given up.'

Daniel's accusations, made weeks ago, burned through Brodie's memory. 'Isn't it about time Drew was free?' he had asked. Free of the responsibility of her, of the old sacrifices—how innocently she had let him extend the dreadful mistake made so many years ago!

Cynthia purred, 'You were a child, then. Somebody had to be responsible for you, and Drew thought it had to be him. But now you're grown, Brodie. You were a nuisance even then, and it won't take much more of this before Drew will see that you still are one. Still standing in the way of his happiness, still grasping for yourself and never counting the cost to others. That's our Brodie.'

'That's not true!' Brodie gasped.

Cynthia shrugged. 'So prove it. Do something nice for Drew.' She didn't have to specify what she had in mind. She pushed her chair back from the dining table and led the way to the living room.

The television set was at a deafening level. In front of it sprawled a little boy surrounded by dirty dishes and candy wrappers.

'Eric,' Cynthia said calmly. There was no response. 'Eric, please.' She called his name several more times, and finally the boy sat up.

'What is it, Mom?' he grumbled. 'You're interrupting my programme.'

'This is my son Eric, Brodie,' Cynthia said. She almost had to shout over the roar of the television. 'Eric, this is Brodie McKenzie.'

'The name,' Brodie said politely, 'is Hammond.'

The glare Cynthia gave her almost shrivelled the wallpaper. She turned back to her son. 'Eric, turn the sound down, please.'

'No.' He sprawled out on the carpet again, selected a biscuit from a crumpled package, and chewed it, brushing the crumbs on to the floor.

'Eric, turn the sound down,' Cynthia repeated.

The boy ignored her.

I wonder if Drew has seen this performance, Brodie wondered.

'Eric!'

He rolled over and grinned. 'I'll turn it down if you promise to buy a set for my room tomorrow,' he bargained.

'Very well,' Cynthia agreed irritably. She picked up his dirty dishes and carried them out of the room.

Eric turned the sound down a fraction. Brodie sat down in the farthest corner of the room. So Cynthia hadn't wanted to be the stepmother of a brat, hmmm? she thought. It ought to be interesting to see Eric get straightened out. She'd bet that any minute now Drew would give Eric the reprimand he deserved. She'd had a few of those herself over the years; she was looking forward to observing.

She closed her eyes and leaned back in the chair, trying a bit of self-hypnosis to block out the laugh track on the comedy programme.

A voice at her elbow asked. 'Are you asleep?'

'I'm sorry,' Brodie said without opening her eyes. 'I can't hear you with that dreadful noise in the background.'

'If you can't hear me,' Eric insisted, 'then why did you answer?'

'I'm so sorry, Eric. I just can't hear you at all.'

A moment later the volume dropped. 'What are you doing?' the voice asked again.

Brodie opened her eyes. 'I was hypnotising myself.'

'Ha! You can't do that. Everybody knows you can't hypnotise yourself!'

'On the contrary,' Brodie said softly. 'It's all self-hypnosis. You have to want to believe, or you can't be hypnotised at all.'

'Really?' Eric sounded suspicious.

'It's very simple, really.' Perhaps I can send the brat off into a permanent trance, she thought wryly.

'Will you teach me?'

'I'll give you a few pointers, if you like. But it requires quiet, so you'll have to turn the television set off.' She closed her eyes again, making it obvious that she didn't care if he co-operated or not.

The noise of the television died. Brodie sat up. 'It works best at first if you're lying down. Later, after a lot of practise——'

'What on earth is going on here?' Cynthia was standing in the doorway.

'She's teaching me to hypnotise myself, Mom.'

Cynthia sounded horrified. 'I will not stand for it,' she said.

'Oh, Mom——' He turned to Brodie. 'Go on. Mom always gives in sooner or later.'

Brodie shook her head. 'Not if your mother disapproves.'

'I certainly do disapprove!' Cynthia heard voices coming down the hall and was suddenly all smiles. 'Eric, here comes Uncle Daniel. Go and greet him like a good boy.'

'Mom!' Eric protested.

'If you want to ever have a television set in your room, Eric——'

So the bribery worked two ways, Brodie thought, suddenly enlightened. She was not surprised, when the men came into the room a couple of minutes later, that Eric was hanging on to Drew's hand, the freckled face smiling as he danced along. And she wasn't surprised that Drew was smiling too. After all, who could resist being charmed by that sweet face?

'I'm disappointed, Drew,' Daniel boomed. 'You were off your game tonight—must have had something else on your mind.' There was a knowing twinkle in his eyes as he looked at Cynthia. 'Didn't you say something about saving dessert for after the game, my dear?'

'Of course, Uncle Daniel. It's my speciality.'

Drew shook his head. 'Sorry, Cynthia. I have a court appearance first thing in the morning. Are you ready to go, Brodie?'

About three hours ago, she wanted to say. But she just nodded.

Cynthia pouted prettily. 'You make sure you get plenty of sleep, Drew,' she told him.

Brodie happened to be watching Eric as his mother cooed over Drew. The child looked disgusted. That makes two of us, Eric, she thought, and felt a sudden spark of sympathy for the child. Brodie knew how it felt to be unwanted, for even though there had always been Drew, it hadn't been like having her own family. There had never been a word breathed to make her feel unwelcome, but she had always known that she didn't really belong with the Hammonds. Yes, she could understand how Eric felt—lonely and deprived and burdensome.

Daniel's house was only a couple of blocks from Safe Harbour, so they had walked over. Now the night was dark and cool, and Brodie shivered a little.

Drew reached for her hand. 'What do you think of Cynthia's little boy?'

'Boys will be boys.' She tried to keep her voice level. My future—what would the relationship be, she

wondered. If Eric's mother married Brodie's guardian
... She shrugged it off. 'Drew, there's something I have
to talk to you about.'

He sighed. 'Not right now, Bro, please? It's a
pleasant night and I'm enjoying a quiet stroll.'

She bit her lip and was silent.

Safe Harbour was dark. 'Can we talk now?' Brodie
asked as soon as they were inside.

Drew turned in the door of the library. 'I have to
review my notes before my court date tomorrow, Bro.'

'I thought you told me that it was routine.'

'If I'm prepared, it will be. But if I'm not certain of
what I want to say, it could turn into a circus. Can't
this discussion wait?'

'I suppose so.' Much as she wanted to get it over,
to tell him straight out that he was free to do as he
liked, there was nothing urgent about announcing it
tonight.

He smiled. 'Thanks, Bro. See you in the morning.'

The door of the library closed with a firm click,
leaving her standing outside. With a deep sigh, she
climbed the stairs to her room.

Once inside she looked around at the bright room
that had been her haven in childhood, and longed for
the days when her hurts had been no more than a cut
finger or a scraped knee, when a bandage could make
anything feel better.

Was Drew too absorbed in tomorrow's business to
talk, or was he afraid of what Brodie would say?——
Afraid, perhaps, that she would argue with him about
Cynthia, try to tell him that he was wrong to still love
her?

Why, she thought, why does everything have to be so
complicated?

It was very early when she woke the next morning after
a night of restless sleep. She was determined not to let
any more time slip away before she talked to Drew, so

she padded down the hall in bare feet to catch him before he left for the office. But his bedroom was empty.

He'd obviously left in a hurry, since the bed was still rumpled, his pillow crooked, the quilted spread askew. She fluffed the pillow and pulled the sheets up square, tucking them in tightly. It made her nervous, to be in his bedroom, and she kept looking over her shoulder as if expecting that he might come back at any moment. As soon as the bed was made, she went back to her own room. She was supposed to work this morning anyway, she concluded. She could talk to him at the office before he went to court.

Sue looked a little doubtful when Brodie told her she had to see Drew. Brodie didn't give her a chance to interfere; she just marched across to Drew's door and knocked.

Once inside, her courage started to desert her. What she had said to herself over and over, rehearsing it in the dark of the night, sounded merely silly in the morning.

'What is it, Brodie?'

'I needed two minutes of your time.' She sat down, her hands clasped tightly in her lap. She started to speak twice, and her voice disappeared. Then she cleared her throat and asked hesitantly, 'Drew, now that Cynthia's going to be free——'

He looked up warily from the transcript he'd been studying. 'What?' he asked cautiously.

'I'm sure that you will want your freedom. I just needed to tell you that it's all right with me.' There. It was said. The hard part was behind her.

He frowned. 'What does that mean, Brodie? Have you decided that you don't want to give our marriage a try?'

'No! That's not——' she stumbled to an unhappy halt.

He watched her in silence for a few moments. Then

he said, very quietly, 'Brodie, the promise I made is a lifelong one.'

'But you said, if I wanted out——'

'I told you that I would let you go.' His voice was low and taut. 'But if you want your freedom, Brodie, you'll have to ask for it. You can't just pretend that you're doing me a good deed. Now if you will pardon me, I am due in court in fifteen minutes.'

He brushed past her and was gone.

She sat there for a long time, her hand over her eyes. She hadn't expressed herself very well, and now he was angry. She should have expected that, Brodie told herself. She was always saying something before she stopped to think of the consequences.

The morning dragged. Sue retreated to her private corner to catch up on her work, leaving Brodie to answer the 'phone and type a brief from Drew's dictated notes. 'At least,' Sue said when they took a brief break, 'with both of them in court it's quiet around here. Cynthia Tandy stays home.'

'Has she been hanging around?' Brodie tried to sound casual.

'All the time,' Sue sighed. 'She's here at least once a day. She says she wants to see Daniel, but when Drew is here, she doesn't pay much attention to her sweet old uncle. And that kid of hers!'

'The brat? She brings him along?'

'Almost every time. He needs a good spanking, just to get his attention, and then some concentrated old-fashioned discipline.'

'You're a dreamer if you think Cynthia will ever give it to him.' Brodie stirred her tea and asked idly, 'How does he behave when Drew is in the room?'

Sue looked thoughtful. 'You know, I hadn't thought about it. But he's almost decent.'

'That figures.' The telephone rang. Brodie pushed her tea aside and answered it.

Drew sounded harried. 'Brodie, I left a stack of

citations on the corner of my desk this morning. Can you bring them down to the courthouse right away?'

'Of course.'

'And bring the Tate file, please. Have Sue dig it out.'

'I can get it.' But he had already hung up.

She found the file in the locked cabinet in his office, where his most confidential papers were kept. As she pulled it out of the bottom drawer, her eye was caught by a file marked 'Tandy'.

'I shouldn't,' she told herself. 'Probably it doesn't have anything to do with Cynthia. Tandy is her married name, after all—if Drew had kept anything of hers it wouldn't be under that name.'

But her fingers seemed to have a mind of their own. The folder slipped out of her shaking hands and dumped its contents on the plush carpet. As Brodie bent to pick up the loose pages and photographs, a phrase in purple ink, in unfamiliar girlish handwriting, jumped out at her. 'Of course I care about you,' it said, 'I will always love you. But I cannot ...' The letter continued on the other side of the delicate stationery, but Brodie didn't turn it over. She pushed it back into the folder with vehemence, along with the photos of a golden Cynthia in brief shorts. She didn't want to know any more, Brodie told herself.

She walked the two blocks to the courthouse in something less than record time, cursing her own curiosity. If Drew had kept Cynthia's letters, her photographs ...

Stop being a fool, she told herself finally. It's not as if you didn't know he still loved her. He had been completely honest about his feelings. It shouldn't matter that he had those mementos tucked away.

But if he still loved Cynthia, she puzzled, then why had he not reached out for his freedom when Brodie offered it?

The answer came quickly. If Drew divorced Brodie, she would be alone again, without a job or anyone to care for her, back where she had been before. So he had refused to consider divorce, because he felt obliged to take care of Brodie.

She had never known before that responsibility could become a bitter taste in the mouth, not only for the one who did the caring, but for the one who was cared for.

The courtroom was quiet except for the voice of an attorney questioning prospective jurors. The rest of the jury panel sat in the back of the big room, waiting with varying degrees of patience to see if they would be needed today.

Brodie found a seat off to the side and let the coolness of the air-conditioned room soothe her hot face. Her overheated thoughts were not so easily disposed of, however.

From her seat, she could see Drew as he listened to each question, his eyes intent on the faces of the jury, noting almost intuitively which ones might be less than fair. No wonder he was so tired after a day in court, Brodie thought, and her heart warmed a bit.

The law was becoming just as fascinating to her as it was to him. She'd been giving a lot of thought lately to Sue's comment that the office needed another paralegal. Was that what she wanted to do?

She had expected that the end of her dreams of a singing career would have felt like a tragedy. But she really hadn't missed it. She certainly didn't miss the smoke and the noisy crowds and the rowdies like Max and his buddies. It was pleasant to have every evening at home, to work in the garden in the cool twilight, to add new dishes to her cooking skills, to sit in the gazebo and watch the sun set behind Safe Harbour, its last rays catching the paned windows and setting the glass aflame with reflected splendour.

She had six music students now. They ranged from Sue's tiny daughter, who could barely stretch her feet to touch the pedals of the grand piano, to a teenager with a dream like Brodie's. The boy was good, too; Brodie hoped that he would find the stamina to go with his talent—the stamina that Brodie lacked.

'Of course you must have talent,' she had told him. 'But unless singing is the most important thing in your life, you'll fail.'

It hadn't been that important to her. For Brodie, the serenity of Safe Harbour had been more valuable. And so she had given up her dream.

The philosophy is nice, she told herself, coming back to the courtroom with a jerk, but it doesn't solve your problem. Thinking about Safe Harbour is pleasant, but you may not have the choice of staying there.

Did she want to be a paralegal? And even if she did, what would happen when Drew wanted to marry Cynthia? She couldn't continue to work in his office then. To see Drew happy because of Cynthia—or worse, to see him unhappy in his marriage—would hurt Brodie deeply. And she was certain that the marriage would not be a happy one. It wasn't Drew that Cynthia wanted, it was the security he represented. And if Brodie had to watch the pain in Drew's eyes when the woman came into the office—or greet Eric calmly when he came in to pester his stepfather . . .

My God, she thought, if Eric starts calling him Dad it will be more than I can bear!

Or to see Drew's own children growing up—assuming that Cynthia would be willing to try motherhood again. Brodie shivered. It was none of her business, but she could not handle it. If that was what Drew wanted, then it was his free choice to make. Despite all the talk of a calm unemotional marriage, perhaps he really preferred the kind of dance Cynthia was sure to lead him.

Love doesn't have to have a reason, Brodie reflected. And as for her, she'd find some other kind of work, and some other town to do it in. Safe Harbour could not be allowed to count.

The attorney finished his questions, and the judge

leaned forward. 'Let's take a five-minute break,' he said. 'Stand up and stretch if you like.'

Drew turned to look for her and beckoned her to come across the courtroom. Brodie put the stack of books on the table. 'Careless of me to forget these,' he said. 'I'm sorry to drag you out in the heat.' His green eyes were searching her face as if he was looking for clues.

'It's all right. I enjoyed the walk.'

'Let's go out to the hall. I have to pick up a transcript at the clerk's office. Shall we go out for lunch, if His Honour recesses soon?'

'Sorry,' Brodie said softly. 'I promised Sue I'd relieve her. She wanted to go home today.' And I'm glad, she thought. With the afternoon to pull myself together, perhaps I'll be all right. But now . . .

'I was going to take you to look at a car. You need one, since I have the Lincoln all the time.'

Brodie shook her head. 'I don't want one, Drew. Really.'

He looked puzzled, but she couldn't find the words to explain that right now she could not accept any more gifts. Her fingers crept to the diamond at her throat and clutched it.

Drew's opponent was also in the hallway. 'Is this a new paralegal, Drew?' he asked, his eyes on Brodie.

'She'd make an excellent one,' Drew told him.

'In that case, I'll try to hire her away from you.'

'It can't be done,' Drew told him. 'This is my wife.'

The attorney was obviously surprised. 'So you finally joined the real world? Why haven't I heard about it?'

'It's only been a week.'

'And you're in court instead of on a honeymoon? What a shame.'

Drew grinned. 'Don't get overconfident, Bill,' he warned. 'Marriage hasn't incapacitated me, you know.'

'I can hope,' Bill laughed, and went back to the courtroom.

The smiling clerk handed Drew a thick sheaf of copy paper. As he flipped through it, Brodie let her eyes roam around the office. She gasped as she caught a glimpse of Jerry, a radiant Isabel at his side, standing at the counter.

Drew had also seen them. 'Applying for their marriage licence,' he said softly.

Brodie looked up through a mist of tears to meet concern in his eyes. 'Does it ever get easier?' she murmured, a break in her voice.

'We don't choose the people we love, Bro.' His tone was solemn. 'Sometimes it just happens, and there is nothing we can do about it.' His hand was gentle as he brushed a loose lock of hair back from her cheek.

It was like an epitaph for his own love. She was thinking about that, and about the tone of his voice as he had introduced her as his wife, while she walked back to the law office. It isn't fair, she was thinking. It isn't fair to Drew, that he is cheated. That's what I'm doing to him. I'm keeping him away from the woman he loves, and I'm giving him nothing in return. If I was really his wife, it would be a little different—but I'm not. I'm just a cheat. Somehow she had to make him believe that she really did want what was best for him. Even if that meant that he married Cynthia.

It seemed to Brodie that the four weeks since she had left school, with Jerry and with such high hopes for the future, had been years and years ago. She was almost twenty-one, and she felt suddenly just about ninety.

CHAPTER TEN

THE week dragged on, and then it slid into another. The case that Drew was trying finished with a victory. One day later he was back in court, and this trial absorbed most of his waking hours. He was always gone when Brodie woke, and he stayed at the office or closeted himself in the library at Safe Harbour till late at night. There was no time to talk to him. In any case, Brodie wasn't certain what it was that she wanted to tell him. She only knew that she was desperately unhappy just now, and she knew that he must be feeling even worse.

The weekend would bring Isabel's wedding day. There had been a frantic hurry about the whole affair, and Brodie couldn't help wondering just who had pushed for a quick wedding. Jerry certainly wouldn't have objected. Isabel was looking forward to being the star of the show, and her father must be desperately anxious to get his problem daughter off his hands. All three of them were in a hurry to get the ceremony behind them.

At any rate, it didn't matter, Brodie told herself. Isabel Fanning's wedding would be the social event of the season in Hammond's Point, and even if the invitations had been mailed just two weeks in advance, instead of the precise month that the etiquette books recommended, the church was certain to be full.

And as the date drew closer, the sense of pressure inside Brodie increased. The rock that seemed to lie in her stomach, the lump that constantly blocked her throat, grew larger with each passing day.

I cannot sit in that church and watch, she told herself despairingly on Friday afternoon, as she sat at her desk in the law office, trying to work on a case file. I cannot observe calmly while the man I love marries another woman, and think about how it should have been me walking down that aisle to meet him, how it should have been our reception, our guests, our honeymoon. I cannot do it.

But she knew she would. There was no excuse big enough to convince Drew that she couldn't go—short, perhaps, of checking herself into the hospital. She wasn't quite up to that.

'What is the matter with you?' Sue asked, late in the afternoon. 'You look like a ghost today.'

Perhaps the hospital idea wasn't so far out of line, Brodie thought wryly. 'I'm just tired of working on this case file.' She put the earplug down and gave the small recorder a push with a contemptuous finger. 'It seems to go on forever.' She was tired of listening to Drew's voice, clipped and firm, as he dictated notes and instructions and summaries of interviews.

Under more normal circumstances, she would probably have been fascinated by the unfolding case and the applicable law. But it was awfully tiresome to listen to Drew's one-sided discussion, especially when he hadn't talked to her about anything else all week, she thought.

'Everything has its boring side, Brodie. The law is no exception.' Sue put down the document she was proofreading. 'What is the matter with you lately? You came in here ready to do anything you were asked and to learn as much as you could. Now, all of a sudden——' She shook her head. 'There doesn't seem to be anything that interests you.'

'I'd really rather not discuss it, Sue.'

But Sue was relentless. 'Are you just bored with working here, or with life in general? Isn't being married as much fun as you expected, Brodie?'

'I am not a child, Sue. I do not expect everything to be sunshine and lollipops, even if that is what you think of me.' Brodie turned back to her work, snapping the

recorder on with an impatient finger. If everyone would
just stop minding my business, I'd be fine, she fumed.

A couple of minutes later Sue leaned over Brodie's
desk and stopped the tape. 'I'm sorry,' she said. 'That
was an unforgivable thing to say.'

Brodie nodded slightly, but she kept her eyes down.

'I can't believe how much better Mr Hammond looks
since you've been married,' Sue went on.

'Do you really think so?' Brodie asked curiously.
'He's been getting out more and playing golf a little
oftener. But he's been so short-tempered all this
week——'

'What do you expect, with two trials in a row like
this? And this one is a stinker.'

Brodie smiled. 'Did you find that description in your
legal dictionary, Sue?'

'It fits. Once it's over and he's done the best he can
for his client, he'll be back to normal.' She paused. 'He
really does look much happier these last few days—
despite the court schedule.'

Since I quit working at the nightclub, Brodie told
herself. And since Cynthia came back.

'I'm sorry I jumped to conclusions that day and told
you he was ill,' Sue mused. 'He must have just been
tired. Now I must get back to work on Isabel's
prenuptial agreement. This is the sixth time we've
written it, because Mr Fanning keeps changing his
mind.'

'He'd better make a decision soon, if the wedding is
still going to be tomorrow.'

'Oh, I fully expect to be running down the aisle
beside Isabel with a fountain pen in my hand.'

'At least he's doing something to protect her,' Brodie
said softly.

Sue looked up in surprise. 'I thought you liked Jerry
Whitcomb.'

Like him? The words were like an arrow into Brodie's
mind. If you only knew, Sue, she thought. 'It just seems

to make sense, when one partner has all the assets, to get an agreement in writing ahead of time.'

'I suppose so. I've never had the problem, so I never gave it a thought.'

'I'm a little surprised that Drew didn't insist on me signing something before he married me,' Brodie mused. 'But then they say that a lawyer who represents himself has a fool for a client—or something like that.'

Sue was absorbed in the contract. 'The cases aren't even similar, Brodie.'

'No.' At least I'm not actively a fortune-hunter, Brodie told herself. Why is it, she wondered, that I can know with every ounce of intelligence I possess that Jerry is bad news, but yet I still love him with every bit of my heart? It's because he had such a rotten childhood, she thought. It hardened him. If he had only had a chance—

Perhaps that's why Drew doesn't want to talk about divorce, she thought idly. If he was the one who wanted his freedom, Brodie could hold him up for quite a settlement. But if he pretended not to care, and she was the one who wanted out—

It doesn't make a shred of difference, she told herself crossly. We made a bad mistake, and it shouldn't have to cost anyone anything. I'm not like Jerry. I don't want to hurt Drew in any way at all, and he ought to know that.

'He doesn't have much to recommend him, does he?' Sue asked idly.

'Who?'

'Jerry Whitcomb. Who else were we talking about?' Sue sounded surprised. 'No money, and from what I hear, not a lot of potential, either. Whereas you have all sorts of possibilities, and the money to carry you through while you try it out. Lucky girl.'

'Drew's money, you mean.'

'No. I mean your trust fund.'

'Not you, too,' Brodie said curtly. 'Everybody in town thinks my father left me a fortune.'

'I'm talking about the trust fund Andy Hammond set up for you,' Sue said gently. 'How much money do you have tucked away, Brodie, if you can't remember an account here and there? I certainly remember it. He was almost as hard to please with that trust as Oliver Fanning has been with this thing.'

The room suddenly seemed to change colour around Brodie. Everything looked pale orange for a minute, and she clenched her hands on the edge of the desk, afraid that she was going to faint.

Sue didn't notice. She continued to scan the neatly typed lines of the prenuptial agreement as she said, 'He wanted you to be independent. He never did take his responsibilities lightly, and once he'd agreed to be your guardian, he thought of you as his own child.'

Why had Drew never told her what his father had done? The question circled in her mind with dizzying speed. Had he broken the trust? or spent all of the money? or gambled it away? The possibilities kept getting wilder and wilder, the longer she thought about it, and none of them made sense. Why had she not known?

She held on to her little remaining poise and said carefully, 'I never did understand trusts, Sue. But now that I know a little more about them, would you explain that one to me?'

Sue looked thoughtful. 'It was pretty standard stuff, Brodie. Nothing unusual or complicated.'

The silence dragged out till Brodie's nerves were stretched to the limit. Then, finally, Sue laid the prenuptial agreement aside with a sigh. 'That's finally done,' she said. 'And a good thing, too, because they'll be here in half an hour to sign it. As for the trust, Brodie, it ended up fairly standard. You start getting the interest when you're twenty-one, the money itself in several payments starting when you're thirty. Or was it twenty-five? That was one of the changes he made, I'm sure. There's a copy around here somewhere.'

I wouldn't bet on it, Brodie thought. 'And in the meantime, Drew could take money out of it for my education, I suppose?'

Sue nodded. 'And anything else you needed. It was pretty liberal about that.'

'Then perhaps it's all been spent.'

The secretary smiled. 'I hardly think that would be possible.' She glanced at the clock. 'It's after five. Go on home, Brodie. I have to stay till the Fannings and Jerry Whitcomb get here, but there's no need for you to stay.'

Brodie absently put away her work. She had no desire to be present when those papers were signed, and she felt a strong need just now to be alone, to think over this stunning news.

On the pavement just outside of the law office, she nearly ran headlong into Isabel Fanning. The girl's arms were full of packages.

'You could watch where you're going, Brodie,' Isabel snapped. 'You nearly knocked me down, and it would have taken forever to pick up all these bags again!'

'Sorry,' Brodie murmured. Their eyes were nearly on a level, Isabel's excited, Brodie's thoughtful. 'Aren't you frightened, Isabel?' she asked suddenly. 'You're marrying a man you've known only a few weeks. It isn't too late to back out, you know—even now.'

Isabel's face froze. 'You'd like that, wouldn't you, Brodie?' she said harshly. 'You still want him, don't you? You're married yourself, now, but you still want Jerry.'

Brodie stumbled over words of denial. How could she possibly explain to Isabel that her concern had nothing to do with her love for Jerry—that she really was frightened for this girl?

'I thought you were my friend,' Isabel said bitingly, and brushed past Brodie to the door.

Heartsick, Brodie climbed the hill to Safe Harbour.

For the first time in her life, though, the house seemed to mock her, to jeer at her instead of welcoming her with open arms. She retreated to the little white gazebo that overlooked the town, and sat there unheeding, her elbows on the small stone-topped table, her head pillowed in her hands, for what seemed hours.

How did it all add up, she asked herself. The trust fund didn't exist now, that was certain, for Drew was incapable of lying about it, even to Jerry. And he had certainly left Jerry with no doubt that Brodie was penniless. So either there had been a trust fund, which had been exhausted by Brodie's needs—a possibility that Sue had found so improbable that it had made her smile—or Andy Hammond had changed his mind at the last minute and not carried through with his plan. That wasn't likely either, Brodie decided, for if he had been so painstaking about writing the document that set up the trust, what could have made him change his mind?

Or had there been a trust that Drew had caused to vanish, either purposely or through mismanagement? Embezzle was a nasty word, Brodie thought, but it was a possibility.

But her mind refused to consider the idea. Drew wasn't capable of such skullduggery. 'Perhaps he broke the trust legally,' she said softly. 'Perhaps there were all kinds of good reasons ...'

But if that was so, why hadn't she known about it? Even if she had been only a child, surely she should have been told! She wanted to stand up and scream out her frustration. There seemed to be no way to find out what had happened, short of asking Drew. And she wasn't certain, just now, whether she'd believe a word he said.

For underneath all the other questions was the one she didn't want to face. Had he married her to cover up a missing trust? If so, not even Cynthia would be reason enough for him to end this marriage.

And, as he had told her days ago, that morning in his office, he would not consider asking for a divorce.

Brodie knew he didn't love her, except perhaps as he would have loved a sister, or a niece. But to be forced to admit that there might not even be fondness in his motives, or caring, or concern—that was too horrible to face.

She waited for him till midnight, sitting in the dimly lit library. By the time the car lights swept past the windows, signalling her that Drew was home, Brodie's fingernails were bitten down to the quick and her body was so tense that she could sit still no longer. She almost ran to the door, determined to have this out as soon as possible.

But the man on the back doorstep, reaching for the bell, was not Drew. 'Jerry!' she breathed. 'What are you doing here?'

'Had to see you,' he said briefly and pushed past her into the kitchen.

'You can't come in. Drew said he'd throw you out in the street if you came here again.'

'He has to catch me first.' Jerry's voice had an odd timbre to it. 'He's still down at his office burning the midnight oil, instead of here taking care of his beautiful bride. Brodie, I can't stand it any more!' He came towards her, arms outstretched.

Brodie dodged away from him.

'I hate to be away from you—I miss holding you, and kissing you, and I go to sleep every night dreaming of making love to you. Brodie, say you still love me. Just let me hear you say it,' he begged.

It was everything she had wanted him to say, and yet—'I'm married, Jerry.' Her voice was dull.

'So will I be, tomorrow. It doesn't have to matter, Brodie. Nothing can come between us. We were made for each other.'

'If you had said those things a month ago——'

'I was stupid,' he said. He caught her in his arms, and Brodie turned her face away to dodge his eager lips. She could smell alcohol on his breath.

'Where have you been, Jerry?'

'At my bachelor party,' he said, and kissed her throat. 'I was celebrating the last night of my freedom, and it suddenly dawned on me—everything I'm giving up. If I could have you, Brodie, it wouldn't bother me at all.'

'I'm terribly flattered,' she muttered. 'Jerry, please let me go.'

'We both know this marriage of yours was a stunt to make me jealous. All right, I admit it—it worked. It's driven me crazy these last two weeks, knowing that you had given Hammond the right to hold you and kiss you and make love to you, when I couldn't. I can't stand it any more, Brodie. Get rid of him!'

'What about Isabel?' she asked quietly. 'You do remember Isabel?'

'It's you I need—it's you I want. Isabel means nothing to me, Brodie. She's a meal ticket for us, that's all.'

She felt ill, afraid that she would collapse right there in his arms before she could get away.

'I wonder how I ever convinced myself that I loved you, Jerry,' she said quietly.

'Because you do,' he said, with delight in his eyes. 'Brodie, darling, we can move the world together. I know we can. Just say you'll be mine——' He bent his head and nuzzled her throat.

'All this time I've told myself that under your hard, disagreeable shell there was a charming little boy, who needed only love,' Brodie mused.

'Your love,' Jerry agreed. 'You're the only one who is important to me.'

'I didn't realise that you were the kind of little boy who finds humour in torturing living things—the kind who has no conscience or concern about other people.'

A scowl appeared on his face. 'Brodie,' he protested, 'that's unkind. The things I've done have all been for us!'

'Including your pursuit of Isabel Fanning?'

He shrugged. 'We have to live somehow.'

'Have you ever heard of working?'

Jerry pressed closer to her, as if by sheer physical presence he could reawaken her feelings. 'Brodie, my darling——' His lips were hot against her throat.

The back door opened. Brodie heard it, and she sucked in a stricken breath, knowing even before she looked up who was standing there. The whole room seemed to freeze.

It was several moments before Drew spoke. 'Isn't this a fascinating little party,' he said, his voice absolutely level. In two strides he had crossed the room, and his left hand clamped on to Jerry's shoulder, pulling him away from Brodie. His right fist connected with Jerry's chin, and Jerry landed with a crash against the edge of Mrs Riley's spotless countertop.

Brodie watched him fall out of the corner of her eye, but her gaze was focused on Drew. She saw the shadow of pain that had flickered across his face as his knuckles connected with Jerry's jaw.

He glanced down at his grazed hand, and said harshly, 'Go to your room, Brodie. This is none of your affair.'

'No.' Her refusal to leave was a mere breath, but it was definite.

'Get out of here. He's been spoiling for this for a month, and he's going to get it.'

'He's drunk, Drew.'

'That's no excuse for his behaviour.'

'It certainly isn't for yours, either.'

His green eyes were fierce. 'As long as we're talking about behaviour, Miss Prim and Proper, we'll discuss your conduct just as soon as I've finished with Mr Whitcomb here.'

'You can't beat up on a drunken man, Drew!'

'If you don't like it, you aren't required to watch.'

She seized his arm, and terror gave her strength to hang on when he tried to shake her off. 'Damn it, Drew, will you stop before you kill him!'

'Right now, I would find it a pleasure.'

Neither of them had been watching as Jerry crept to his feet. Brodie saw him first, with the very fringe of her vision, as he picked up a heavy glass fruit bowl and dumped its contents on the counter.

'Watch out, Drew!' she shrieked.

Drew wheeled around and his upraised forearm caught Jerry's, sending the bowl spinning to the floor in a million fragments. This time Drew's fist drove into Jerry's stomach. As Jerry went down, his head thudded against a cabinet door.

The silence in the room was complete for the first few seconds. Then Jerry's eyes fluttered open, and Brodie slowly released the breath she had been holding.

Drew's eyes were humourless. 'Your prayers have been answered, my dear,' he said. 'I didn't kill him after all. As hard-headed as he is, I doubt that I've even hurt him. He may think tomorrow that he has an unusually bad hangover, but he's probably used to that.'

Brodie's voice was low and tight. 'As far as I'm concerned, you can both go to hell.' She fought off tears as she ran up the stairs to the safety of her bedroom.

She was shaking so hard that she could scarcely close the door, and she stood in the centre of the room trembling for several minutes, too upset even to sit down. The horror of what had happened down in the kitchen—and worse, the horror of what could have come about—made her feel ill.

There had been murder in Drew's eyes. She had never seen it before, had never believed that a sane, responsible human being could be pushed to that point.

But it had been there tonight, and she had been terrified.

Finally her nerves calmed enough so that she was no longer on the point of screaming. I must go talk to him, she thought, and before she could argue herself out of it, she shakily descended the stairs.

He was in the library, staring out of the Gothic windows across the dark garden. She stood in the doorway for several minutes before he turned and saw her.

'If you're looking for the boyfriend, he left. Under his own steam, though he was weaving a little on his way to the car.'

'I thought he was you, when he drove in. I would never have opened the door if I'd known it was Jerry.'

He didn't answer.

'I swear I'm telling the truth, Drew!'

Still there was silence. Drew had turned back to the window and didn't give a sign that he had even heard her.

She picked up the black king from the chess set at her elbow and threw it at him. 'Damn it, Drew, will you listen to me?' She was almost screaming.

He turned then. 'Why should I, Brodie? Why should I listen and let you try to wheedle me into believing that black is white? You can tell me whatever you want in that sweet little voice of yours—about how you didn't invite him and you didn't want him to be here. And I still won't believe it.'

Brodie swallowed hard. 'I'll talk to you tomorrow,' she said then. 'Perhaps by then you can be reasonable about it.' She crossed the hall and started to climb the stairs.

'I think I'm being very reasonable,' he said as he followed her. 'I've taken all the nonsense I'm going to take.' He was advancing on her, coming up the stairs with measured, slow step.

'I didn't invite him here,' she whispered. She retreated against the wall at the head of the staircase.

'But you certainly let him hold you, didn't you?' He braced his hands on the wall above her shoulders, and then let them slide slowly down till the warmth of his fingers burned into her arms. 'Like this, Brodie? And I'm sure he kissed you.'

'I tried to stop him,' she breathed.

'As you're trying to stop me now?' he asked, very softly, against the pulse that beat wildly at the base of her throat. His lips were gentle, unlike the harsh words, sliding up the silken skin to the triangle under her ear. He pushed the dark hair back and nibbled her earlobe. 'Is that how you tried to stop him?'

'I did try,' she whispered.

'And then did he do this?' Drew's hand slid down over her shoulder to cup her breast for a moment, and then, as if the momentary contact had only made him want more, his long fingers began to unbutton her blouse. In moments, the fabric had been pushed out of his way, and he was toying with the creamy skin that peeked out from the lacy cup of her bra.

'No,' she said, but her voice trembled.

Drew's mouth found hers, and the contact was scorching. Brodie tried to pull away, but he would not let her go. 'How far has it gone, Brodie?' he asked, his voice very soft. 'Have you been to bed with him yet, or is that treat still ahead of us all?'

'Drew——'

His eyes were blazing as he raised his head. 'If I'm going to have the honour of giving my name to your first-born child, Brodie, then I'd like for there to at least be a chance that it's actually mine. That seems fair enough, doesn't it?' He reached around her and turned the doorknob, then picked her up and carried her the few steps to her bed. He tossed her down into the middle of the bed and stood for a moment looking at her. Then, before she could roll away from him, or even protest, he was beside her.

He had kissed her like this once before, she thought,

at the hotel on that dreadful night when the rowdies had tried to attack her. That night he had merely been illustrating the danger she was in. Was he perhaps doing the same thing tonight? If she relaxed and played along, would he eventually just laugh and let her go and tell her to be more careful in the future?

'Drew——'

'I'm glad you remember my name,' he said, against her lips. He had pinned her down to the bed with the length of his body holding her there, helpless, and he played with her as if she was a new toy. Her breath was coming in gasps that hurt her throat. His long fingers were gentle against her bare breast. He toyed with her, but his mouth was harsh as it moved across her throat, her cheek, then returned to her lips, this time to demand a response.

My God, he means to go through with this, she thought, and panic threatened to choke her. With her last fragment of strength, she turned her head away and gasped, 'Not like this, Drew. Oh, my God, Drew, not like this!'

He tensed, every muscle in his body taut. Brodie held her breath, waiting, knowing that whatever he said or did, she had no more strength to resist him. Then he sighed.

'No,' he said, very quietly. 'Not like this.' His fingers brushed her cheek and her slender arm. She could see a tiny bruise beginning to form next to the rosy tip of one delicate breast. He pressed his lips to it, very gently, and laughed without humour when she pulled away, unable to lie there quietly.

'I will not hurt you again,' he said, and his voice was full of pain.

Then he was gone, and she was alone in the silent night.

CHAPTER ELEVEN

SLEEP eluded her. Whenever she closed her eyes, she could again feel the heat of Drew's hands caressing her body, and she would sit up straight, wide-eyed, looking around to be certain that she was alone, to be sure that it was only her imagination which tormented her.

She was shivering, despite the blankets under which she huddled. She knew, however, that it was not cold that caused her discomfort, but the bitter realisation of what had almost happened.

'If you're going to play games with the big boys,' she told herself. 'you'd better be prepared to take care of yourself.'

Not even Drew could always be trusted. For Brodie, it was a bitter admission. The Drew she had seen tonight was not the one she had known for all these years. She had never suspected that he was capable of violence; for Drew there had always been a peaceable way to settle every problem.

She pushed back the blankets and paced the floor for what seemed hours, tormenting herself with the evening's events. If she hadn't let Jerry come in, she thought—that's where the problem started. Or was it when she had gone back down to talk to Drew? If she hadn't done that, would it have been all right? What single action, which word, had set off the explosive blast that would destroy her world?

It had been destroyed, there was no question of that. No matter what Drew had said, she could not stay here now. Safe Harbour was no longer the peaceful sanctuary of her childhood, if she was not protected in her own bedroom.

'And you're no longer a child, either,' she told herself

firmly. 'So stop feeling sorry for yourself.' That was where the problem had started, she thought. You can't be grown up, and married, and playing adult games with real human emotions, and expect things to stay as simple as they had been all those years ago. You can't be married to one man, and in love with another, and not get into trouble.

In love. Well, that was one more dream down the drain, she thought, and sighed. She supposed that she should be glad. Since she could not ever have Jerry, she should feel happy to have discovered that she really hadn't wanted him under any circumstances.

'I was in love with the idea of being in love,' she told herself, without emotion. 'Not with Jerry.'

She was vaguely surprised to see that she had not worn a path in the deep pile of the carpet with her pacing. She sat down at her dressing table and began to brush her hair, feeling that if she didn't do something with her hands she might just start to throw things.

She supposed that she should feel shocked at her own stupidity in getting involved with Jerry, or relieved that Isabel Fanning, and not she, was the one to be caught in his grand design. But she felt only emptiness. The love that had been the centre of her existence for so long had gone out of her life, and now there was nothing to replace it.

Even the half-life that Drew had offered, with the marriage that might someday be more than a travesty, was denied to her now. 'I could never trust him again,' she said. 'Not after what happened tonight.'

But nothing happened, her other self argued. Drew could have overpowered her, forced himself on her. But he hadn't. The merest word of protest from her had brought him back from the boundaries of that shadowy, terrifying violence, back to the Drew she knew and loved.

Loved? Her breath came in a harsh gasp, and her

hand clenched on the handle of the brush so tightly that her knuckles were white. Loved?

'I love him as a brother,' she said breathlessly, talking to her white-faced reflection in the mirror. 'I love him as an uncle—as a father——'

But as a husband? She shook her head, but the ghost in the mirror seemed to stare back at her, unmoved by her protest.

Then why did you marry him? The question seemed to ricochet around the room.

'Because I was lonely,' she said, defensively. 'Because I was afraid to go out in the world by myself. Because he asked me to do this one thing for him, and I wanted to please him and make him happy——'

And isn't that what love is? Wanting his happiness, even at the cost of your own? The questions assaulted her from all sides.

'No,' she protested. 'Love is more than that. It's that crazy, giddy feeling that makes the world look rosy. It's wanting to be with someone so much that nothing else matters. Love—real love—makes all the other problems go away. If two people love each other enough, then nothing can hurt them, nothing can come between them. And it lasts forever. That's the kind of feeling that I had for Jerry——'

But it wasn't, she admitted painfully. For what she had thought was love hadn't made the problems go away. The practical matters hadn't vanished, just because they had declared themselves to be in love.

And it hadn't lasted, once she had seen Jerry for what he really was. Her definition was wrong, then.

She planted her elbows on the dressing table and dropped her face into her hands. 'Love is working together, and making a home, and having children and building a life——' This was dangerous ground, she told herself. She stopped abruptly, and started over again. 'Love has to include passion,' she said firmly, delighted that she had found a way to talk herself out of this ridiculous notion. Being in love with Drew—indeed!

'If there isn't that spark of physical desire, that hunger to be a part of the other person, then it isn't really love.' That was simple enough, she decided. And that was what was missing from her feelings for Drew.

She got back into bed, certain that—with her problem solved—sleep would now come quickly. Tomorrow would be time enough to figure out where she could go, what she would do next.

But the instant her eyes closed, she could feel the warmth of his hands again, the taste of his kisses, the hard strength of his body as he had held her.

A footstep sounded on the hardwood floor of the hallway, just outside her door. She sat up straight, eyes wide.

'Brodie?' His voice was scarcely more than a whisper. 'Are you awake?'

She held her breath, afraid that any sound might betray her. There was a long silence outside her room, and then his steps faded away down the hall, and his bedroom door closed with a gentle click that seemed to echo through the silent house.

It was oddly final. She knew, somehow, that he would not be coming back. Brodie released her breath in a sigh, and lay back, clutching her pillow, tears streaming down her face.

The passion was there, she knew, finally admitting what her heart had known for weeks—perhaps for much longer than that. When she thought of Drew, it wasn't as a guardian or an uncle, it was as a lover. It had been that way at least since the night in her hotel room when she had, underneath her confusion, wanted him to stay with her. His kisses—his very touch that night—had roused a flame in her, and a deep curiosity. The feeling had frightened her so much that she had tried to deny that it even existed, and yet at the same time it had drawn her irresistibly back to him.

She had protested, tonight, when he had tried to make love to her, but she had not fought him. She had not been revolted by his touch. 'Not like this,' she had said, and Drew had left her. And part of her had been sorry that he had gone.

If he had come to her in gentleness, and not with that breath of violence still hovering about him, she would have welcomed him. 'Because I love him,' she murmured, and pressed her hands against hot cheeks.

Love, she thought with sudden new awareness. 'It's sharing the pain as well as the joy,' she said, and didn't mind at all that she sounded a bit maudlin, 'because it isn't possible to have a life without pain. It's crying together as well as laughing, because there will be sadness. It's sharing, and caring, and fighting, and playing—all those things that I want to spend my life doing . . .' She hesitated, and took a deep breath. 'With Drew,' she whispered, and wished with all the strengh at her command that she had not protested and sent him away. If she had held him, and been gentle with him, he would have returned that gentleness, and now she would be his wife in fact, sharing with him a relationship that even Cynthia could never share . . .

Cynthia. In the emotional storm that she had been battling. Brodie had forgotten about Cynthia, and about why she had been waiting in the library for Drew to come home.

She slid out of bed and curled up on the window seat, staring out over the city lights. She tried to feel again the hurt she had felt when Sue had told her about the trust fund, but somehow it didn't seem to matter any more. It would have to be settled, though, she thought sadly. She would ask him about it tomorrow, and then she would decide what to do.

And if her suspicions were right, if there was no fund, and if he had indeed married her so that missing money could be concealed, then—'I don't want to know,' she whispered, burying her face in a satin cushion.

Love is wanting so much for him to be happy that you're willing to sacrifice your own happiness. The words seemed to echo inside her head. But if his happiness meant that she must set him free to marry Cynthia . . .

'I can't do it,' Brodie said, and her voice was curt in the dark room. 'I cannot let him go, now.'

She sat there on the windowseat, wide-eyed and sleepless, her forehead pressed against the cool glass.

Three o'clock came—the hour when stamina is lowest, when the night is so deep and long that it seems impossible for the sun ever to rise again. It found Brodie still sitting there by the window, waiting for the dawn, fighting a battle within herself.

Then, very slowly, like a sleepwalker, she rose, stretched muscles stiffened by the long night, and went to find him. The longest hour in Brodie's life, the hour of doubt and waiting, was past.

The big front bedroom was quiet, and dark except for the moonlight which trickled through the open windows. For a moment, she thought he was asleep, and she almost seized the opportunity to retreat. Then he spoke from the shadow, and Brodie gasped.

'Why did you come here, Bro?' It was soft, almost as if he doubted that she was really there.

Brodie took a deep breath and silently crossed the room. 'This is something I have to do.'

He raised up on one elbow. 'Brodie, don't you understand?' he said, his voice husky. 'I tried to rape you. You don't owe me anything, my dear—not even politeness—after that.'

'Perhaps it's something that I owe myself, Drew.' She stood there in the moonlight, feeling awkward and naïve and unbearably gauche. Then she whispered, 'Will you make love to me now?'

'Why, Brodie?'

She sat down on the edge of the bed and reached out with a shaky hand to touch his face. His stubbly dark beard scratched her tender fingertips. 'I don't want to talk tonight, Drew. Please——' There was the thread of a sob in her voice. 'If we could just pretend——'

There was a long silence, and she thought dizzily that he was going to reject her.

'God help me,' he said quietly, 'but I am not strong enough to send you away.' He held out a hand.

Brodie crept into his arms. His skin was warm and supple under her cheek as he cradled her, holding her close. 'I'm afraid,' she whispered.

'You needn't be,' he said. His hands were gentle, his mouth tender as he caressed her. Her first sensation was surprise, and then wonder, as a flicker of passion kindled deep within her and grew to a flame that threatened to consume her.

I never, never expected it to be like this, she thought. I can't be alone in feeling this way. And she knew with her last coherent thought that Drew shared every instant of ecstasy and triumph as they reached together for the heights, and drifted back to earth on a slow, lazy cloud.

'Still nothing to say?' he murmured finally, his lips warm against the curve of her throat.

Brodie shook her head. What could there be to talk about, she wondered. Their bodies had said it all so well without words.

Drew drifted off to sleep then, his face buried in her hair, and a kind of exhausted peace dropped over her— the peace that comes to a woman when she has fought her last battle, and surrendered.

But peacefulness fled with the coming of the morning light. When the first rays of sunshine peeked in the windows. Brodie stirred, and remembered, and was horrified by what she had done.

Drew still slept, sprawled on his back with one arm flung up over his head. Brodie watched him through narrowed eyes.

I must have been crazy, she thought, to have done such a thing. What could have been wrong with me, to come to his room at that awful hour of night and beg him to make love to me?

And, after all was said and done, what difference did it make? There was still the trust fund, there was still Cynthia. All Brodie had done was to complicate things with this child's trick.

As if sleeping together could be the answer to anything! She inched out of the bed, holding her breath, careful not to do anything which might awaken him. She had to search for her nightshirt, found it discarded on the carpet, and slipped out of the room with a sigh of relief. It would be embarrassing enough to meet him downstairs; to be still in his bed when he woke would be more than she could stand.

She sat in the kitchen drinking coffee until her nerves began to unravel, wondering what he would say when he came down. If he was upset with her, she didn't know how she would be able to hold up her head. But it would be even worse if he was to feel sorry for her.

The clock edged on inexorably, and still Drew did not appear. When less than an hour remained till Isabel's wedding would begin, she poured his coffee and slowly climbed the stairs.

There was no answer when she tapped on the bedroom door; she pushed it open. 'Drew?' she said, and looked around. The room was empty, the sheets still in a haphazard pile in the middle of the bed. A slow, embarrassed blush rose over her as she looked at the wreckage left from last night.

The hiss of water in the shower died abruptly, and she called, 'Drew? Don't forget that the wedding is at ten.'

'I'll be there in a minute.'

Her nerve deserted her, and she left his coffee on the bedside table and retreated to her room. Suddenly it seemed very important that she look her best today; she searched through her wardrobe and finally chose a mustard-coloured dress. It draped around her slender figure and made a perfect background for the diamond necklace that she put on today almost as a shield. She hurried through her make-up, tucked her hair up in a twist, leaving only a few tendrils loose around her face, and added a wide-brimmed ivory straw hat. It made her look older and more elegant, she thought. And besides, the brim shaded her face. It would make it more difficult to anyone to read her thoughts.

Drew was waiting her for at the bottom of the stairs. Her heart twisted as she saw him there. He was as handsome as she had ever seen him, in a well-tailored light grey suit.

As she reached the bottom step, he looked into her eyes, level with his, and said, 'Good morning, Brodie.' His eyes were brilliant green and watchful, and she could read no expression into his voice.

Apparently he was not going to mention the insanity of the night. Very well, Brodie thought, neither will I. She glanced into her handbag to be sure she'd picked up her make-up kit and said with composure, 'We'll have to hurry.'

There was a long silence before he said, 'What a shame it would be to miss the wedding of the century.' Was there the merest hint of sarcasm in his tone?

'I'm certain it will be worth seeing.'

'Especially for you,' he said, and there was no longer any doubt about the sarcasm. 'If you didn't see Jerry married, you probably wouldn't believe he'd actually gone through with it.'

She didn't answer. He locked the front door behind them and said in a much different tone, 'I'm sorry, Bro. That was uncalled for.'

She steadied the trembling of her hand, and laid it as calmly as she could on his sleeve. I'm going into the church on my husband's arm, she told herself. And no one but the two of us need know, today, what a mess we've made of it.

It was just a block from Safe Harbour to the grey stone church, and the bells were already pealing joyfully as they left the brilliant sunlight for the cool dimness of indoors. It took Brodie's eyes a moment to adjust. Then, as she saw the banks of flowers on the altar, and the candles already burning, it seemed for the first time to be real. Jerry and Isabel were actually going to be married today. Automatically she braced herself against the pain, her fingers digging into Drew's arm. But the ache that had been ever-present since that moment when Jerry had told her the truth had gone, leaving behind only a sort of grey, dull emptiness. With a deliberate effort, she relaxed.

Mercifully, it was only moments till the rich tones of the organ began to fill the church, letting her lose herself in the music. She watched as Isabel came up the aisle on her father's arm, the sparkle of triumph in her eyes lending animation to the little face. And she noticed, disinterestedly, that Jerry looked pale, and that the side of his face was a bit puffy. She wondered if he even remembered today that he had come to Safe Harbour last night.

'Dearly beloved,' the minister said, and Brodie closed her eyes, losing herself in memories of her own wedding day, little more than two weeks ago. Then she had paid scant attention to the majestically simple words. Now she let them flow over her, drinking in the ages-old magic that melded two separate people into one.

I, Jerry, take thee, Isabel, to be my wedded wife . . .' Jerry's voice was quiet, but firm, as he repeated his vow.

Drew's hand tightened on Brodie's, and she knew that he was watching her, wondering if she could bear up under this burden. She kept her head tilted down, the brim of the hat shading her face from his searching eyes.

'To have and to hold from this day forward . . .'

How could Drew sit there, holding her hand, and remain unaware of the change in her, she wondered. Couldn't he somehow feel the difference?

'For better, for worse . . .'

But he must remain unaware, she reminded herself. That had been their deal. They had agreed to an unemotional, safe, secure partnership. It had been no part of their plans for Brodie to tumble headlong into love.

'For richer, for poorer . . .'

I wouldn't count on that one, Isabel, Brodie thought.

'In sickness and in health . . .'

She remembered the fear that had clutched her that day when Sue had shared her suspicions that Drew was ill. Brodie had been horrified at the thought of losing him. Even then, she knew, her love had been hiding just under the surface of her mind. Older and wiser now, she could recognise the signs.

'To love, honour and cherish . . .'

How mortifying it would be if Drew ever realised what had happened to her. Even if he wanted to be free, then, he would feel honour bound to her. For Drew was the essence of an honourable man.

Brodie felt the hot tears stinging her eyelids, and drew a deep breath, trying to fight them off. Drew's hand tightened on her fingers again until she almost cried out. It was just as well that he thought she was crying for Jerry, she told herself. If he knew that her tears were for herself, and for the vow she had made just two weeks ago, he would probably laugh at her sentimentality. Or, worse, he would not laugh—just quietly sacrifice his own happiness for hers.

Perhaps he wouldn't even believe that she knew what she was feeling. After all, she was the one who had insisted that her love for Jerry would be lifelong, that no one could ever take his place. How could she expect Drew to believe, just days later, that she had changed?

'Until death do us part . . .'

Brodie heard Jerry say the words, and she wondered about herself. Would it be forever, for them? Or would their marriage be like so many others, ending in a cold courtroom, perhaps without either of them even present to mourn its passing?

Not if I have anything to say about it, Brodie thought determinedly. If it ends, it will be because Drew wants it that way.

Drew had said his vows would be lifelong. But had he really meant it on that hot Sunday morning, when he had made these same promises to Brodie? Or had he, like Jerry, been a little selective about what he would do? Would Cynthia win out after all?

How humorous it was, Brodie thought, that the marriage which she had intended merely to soothe her broken heart had suddenly become so tragically important. They had set out to find what happiness they could, together, in an unhappy world. Now Brodie knew with deep certainty that if she could not have Drew she wanted no one else. I'd rather be lonely than to try to find comfort with someone else, she thought. She hadn't felt that way when Jerry had rejected her. Funny, how much different things looked now.

Long before she was expecting it, the organ pealed forth again, and Jerry and Isabel came back down the aisle, Isabel was all smiles, and they were almost running.

Someone had once told Brodie that every bride was beautiful on her wedding day, and she realised abruptly how true it was of Isabel. I wonder, Brodie thought, if I was beautiful too, or if it is love shining out of a girl's eyes on her wedding day that makes the difference. I hope Isabel is still wearing that look in a year, she thought. I hope it works out for them.

'Are you all right?' Drew murmured.

She nodded.

'I know how hard this is for you. I don't want to make it any harder——'

Cynthia linked her arm in Drew's. 'Quite a splash, wasn't it?' she said cheerfully. 'And wasn't it fascinating how the crowd split so neatly? All the country-club set on this side of the church, to avoid being contaminated by the groom's friends.'

Trust Cynthia to notice something like that, Brodie thought. She kept her head down.

Daniel pulled Drew aside. 'How is the trial going?' he asked, and they stepped off to the side to talk about it.

'You look dejected, little one,' Cynthia added with phoney sympathy. 'Is it because you weren't asked to sing? Or are you sorry that Isabel's wedding, and not yours, was the social event of the year? You shouldn't be.'

'I'm not,' Brodie denied softly.

Cynthia wasn't convinced. 'This one can't last, you know. And just think how embarrassed Isabel is going to be when the marriage breaks up before she's written her thank-you cards.'

'You can't know that,' Brodie pointed out. 'They might be very happy together.'

'Are you offering odds?' Then Cynthia returned to the attack. 'At least you'll be spared that. You should be glad you had more sense than to insist on a splash. A quiet wedding, a quiet divorce, and it will be just as if it never happened.'

Brodie looked up then, into Cynthia's bright blue eyes. 'And what makes you think Drew and I will get a divorce?'

Cynthia laughed, triumphantly. 'Drew married you out of desperation, so that I wouldn't think he was still in love with me. It was rather charming of him—like a small boy trying to hide. But the moment he found out that I'll soon be free, you didn't stand a chance, Brodie.'

'You're very certain of yourself.'

'Of course. Oh, I quite realise that it may take a little while for him to soothe his conscience about you. Drew's moral convictions are one of the sweetest things about him. But I'm in no hurry. He'll soon get tired of playing your games, and then he'll come back to me.'

'You make it sound inevitable.' Brodie tried to keep her voice level. 'As if I have nothing to say about it.'

'You don't, honey. Admit it. You can't hold a man who doesn't want to be held.' Her eyes were cold.

I'm certainly going to try, Brodie told herself. And then we'll see, Cynthia. We will see.

CHAPTER TWELVE

THEY were brave words. But in the next few days, Brodie could find no way to make them work. The silence inside Safe Harbour deepened as each day went by, until even the house itself seemed sullen and withdrawn. Drew spent most of his waking hours at the office, working on the trial that had now dragged into a second week. When he was home he was in his library. And Brodie was like a ghost, quiet and sleepless, searching for a peace of mind that avoided her.

Could there be any chance for their marriage to survive? There were days when they hadn't exchanged even a dozen words. What hope did they have of any lasting peace? The question grew to haunt her as the days dragged on.

She was giving a piano lesson to Sue's daughter on that Wednesday afternoon. June's heat had fallen like a wet, smothering fog Hammond's Point, and a summer thunderstorm threatened. Though it was cool inside Safe Harbour, the dark sky and the falling air pressure outside made the big drawing room seem like a cave into which she had crawled to lick her wounds.

'Try it again,' she told the child, and braced herself to listen to Three Blind Mice for the fourth time that afternoon. It really was a sin, she thought, to subject that priceless antique grand piano to the tiny, uncertain fingers of a child! And yet her students loved it. It seemed to hold a magical attraction for them that no ordinary piano could.

Mrs Riley came down the hall. 'Your friend Isabel is here,' she said curtly. 'I put her in the morning room.'

Brodie thought for a moment that she'd heard

wrong. 'Isabel was going to Jamaica for a week,' she pointed out.

'I don't know anything about her plans. I just know she's here, now.'

'Offer her a cup of tea. I'll be there in a minute.' Brodie assigned her pupil's next lesson, rewarded her performance with a biscuit fresh from Mrs Riley's oven, and waved goodbye from the front door as the little figure, in raincoat and tall boots, started for home. Then she went to the morning room, wondering uneasily what was in store for her now. It must be something dreadful to have brought Isabel back early from her honeymoon. Had Jerry got drunk and told her all those awful things he had said to Brodie the night before his wedding—that Isabel was a meal ticket, that she meant nothing to him, that Brodie was his only love? If that had happened, then Isabel might do anything. Brodie wondered uneasily if she should tell Mrs Riley to call Drew, or the police.

No, she thought, and told herself firmly to stop being melodramatic. She couldn't bother Drew. He was in court, hoping that his case would go to the jury this afternoon. And surely there was no need for police protection, from little Isabel!

Isabel was standing by the curved bay window, as if she could not bear to be confined to a chair. She was wearing dark glasses, and she stared out across the town, presenting only a profile to the room. What Brodie could see of her face, around the heavy frames of the glasses, was pale—hardly what she would have expected after even a few days in the Caribbean sun.

Brodie waited quietly while Mrs Riley arranged the tea trolley. Then she said, 'Thank you. I'll pour.'

Isabel hadn't seemed to hear her come in, for she hadn't looked away from the window. But when the door had closed behind the housekeeper, she said, 'You knew what would happen, didn't you?'

Brodie was honestly confused. 'Knew what, Isabel?'

'Just do me one favour, Brodie. Don't say, "I told you so"—all right?' Without waiting for an answer she wheeled away from the window and pulled off the dark glasses.

Brodie gasped. Isabel's left eye was swollen nearly shut, the lid purple. The bruising extended down the side of the girl's face and back into her hair.

'That's not all,' Isabel said curtly. She pushed up her sleeve to show another bruise, this one faded to yellow. 'There are more, if you'd like to see them.' She clutched at her side, as if taking a deep breath hurt her.

'Your ribs, too?' Brodie asked quietly.

Isabel nodded grimly. 'I think one may be broken. At least, I've never felt this sort of pain before.'

'Then perhaps you'd better not have any tea until you've seen a doctor.'

'It happened three days ago, Brodie. I've been eating ever since—when I felt like it. I haven't been very hungry,' she admitted.

'It didn't all happen three days ago,' Brodie said quietly. The bruises were in all stages of healing; they had not all been inflicted at one time. It didn't take a professional to know that this had been no isolated incident.

Isabel shrugged, and a wince crossed her face. 'No. The eye was last night—that was what tore it. When he went out to the beach this morning, I packed up and ran. I may be dumb, Brodie, but I know this much—I don't have to be my husband's punching bag.'

'You certainly don't.' Brodie sat down in a white wicker chair, put her head back against the yellow cushion, and said, 'I don't mean to sound rude, Isabel, but why did you come to me?'

'Because you really seemed to care that day when you saw the bruise on my arm. Besides, I didn't want to walk into Mr Hammond's office looking like this. It was bad enough that your housekeeper saw me.'

'She's very discreet.' Brodie toyed with the teapot.

'Drew is in court. I don't know when he'll be home, and I think you need medical care, Isabel.'

'Well, give me a cup of tea and we'll talk about it.' She sat down and tossed the glasses on to the table. 'I'm going to get an annulment, of course.'

Brodie picked up a delicate china cup and saucer. She felt no triumph, no relief—nothing much at all, in fact. 'Have you talked to your father?'

'No. That pleasure is still ahead of me.'

'You'll have to tell him sometime, Isabel. Surely when he sees you like this——'

The girl was shaking her head. 'I wouldn't count on it,' she said, with an edge to her voice. 'But I suppose I have to try.'

'You'll need his backing.'

Isabel's eyes were like those of a hunted animal. 'Would you call him? I'm so scared of him—I'm sorry that I'm imposing on you, but I didn't know what else to do.'

'I think it would be better if you called.' Brodie set her cup down with a firm click. 'Would you like me to leave you alone?' She didn't wait for an answer, and as she left the room, Isabel was reluctantly reaching for the telephone.

Someday you're going to be in serious trouble for minding someone else's business, Brodie told herself. When it came to Oliver Fanning, there were no guarantees. Little wonder, she thought, that Isabel was afraid of the man!

A few minutes later, Isabel came to find her in the drawing room. 'It's all right,' she said, a note of wonder in her voice. 'Daddy's going to call the doctor, and meet me at the hospital, Brodie!'

I can't believe it, Brodie told herself. One thing that I've meddled in might turn out all right. At any rate, I owe it to Isabel to try to patch things up. If it hadn't been for me, she might never have got involved with Jerry.

The girl seemed to relax. 'Someone should have warned us that being married isn't all fun,' she said. 'You aren't having an easy time of it either, are you?'

Brodie murmured something indistinct.

'I thought when Cynthia Tandy first came to town that it was kind of funny to see you squirm,' Isabel mused. 'You'd always had everything, and it was amusing to see that you had problems too.'

'I understand,' Brodie said. 'I'll tell Drew that you want to see him.'

'Yes. Daddy thought the annulment was a good idea.' She gave Brodie an impulsive hug, and was gone.

That was one thing that was going to straighten itself out, Brodie thought. In a way, she was envious of Isabel. At least the girl knew where she was going now.

The storm burst furiously over Hammond's Point, and then, in the manner of summer thunderstorms, it passed by, leaving the air cool and crisp. The garden looked as if it had been washed clean, the colours bright and sharp.

Brodie was sitting on the terrace, sipping iced tea, when Drew came home. She was surprised when the Lincoln pulled into the drive, for she hadn't expected him to be home for dinner at all. She'd even sent Mrs Riley home. There was no point in her fixing a meal that Brodie wouldn't eat.

When he reached the drawing room a few minutes later, he poured himself a glass of wine from the trolley, and joined her on the terrace. He looked tired. 'The trial is over,' he said.

'How did it turn out?' Brodie knew there was no interest, no animation, in her voice. Right now she couldn't force herself to feel any enthusiasm.

'Do you care?' Drew asked sombrely. Before she found an answer, he added. 'They offered a settlement right before the case went to the jury. My client took it.'

'That's good. But all that time and work wasted——'
She swirled the ice in her empty glass. 'Drew—how
hard is it to get an annulment?'

The delicate stem of his glass snapped in his hand,
and wine splashed over the tile floor. Drew swore and
brushed a few drops off his trousers. 'Very difficult,' he
said finally. 'Why do you ask?'

'Isabel is home.' Brodie set her glass aside. 'She wants
out of her marriage.'

There was a long silence. 'She may have to settle for a
divorce,' he said. 'Annulments aren't easily come by
unless there was fraud, or one partner was under age.
Bad judgment doesn't make good legal grounds. Would
you like more tea?'

'Please.' She handed him her glass and watched
through the open terrace doors as he poured more wine
for himself. 'So Isabel's fairy-tale marriage lasted less
than a week,' he said over his shoulder.

'It could have been expected,' Brodie said. She shifted
her lawn chair to better catch the cool breeze.

'By everyone except Isabel, that is,' he said. 'What
happened, anyway?'

'Jerry beat her up.'

Drew handed her the icy glass. She was breathlessly
aware of his touch. She'd been so careful in the last few
days to stay out of his way, because any contact sent
her heart racing as she remembered that crazy night.
How utterly silly, she thought.

'You're no doubt wondering what she did to provoke
him,' he suggested coolly.

Brodie's mouth dropped open. 'Of course I'm not.
Drew, of all the sexist remarks—I could throw
something at you. There's never any excuse for a man
who puts bruises on his wife!'

There was dead silence on the terrace for two full
minutes. Brodie bit her lip, not daring to look directly
at him. But out of the corner of her eye, she could see
that he was as still as a statue, and she knew that he was

thinking of that night, too, and of the bruises he had left on her.

Finally he sighed heavily. 'You're right, Brodie. I deserved that.'

She played with the slice of lemon on the rim of her glass and said quietly, 'It wasn't aimed at you. What happened between us was different.'

'Was it?' he asked. 'When you asked about the annulment, I thought perhaps it was you who wanted it, Brodie.'

Tears rose in her eyes. She dashed them away, refusing to look at him.

'I understand, Bro,' he said gravely. 'I made a mistake, I am sorry, my dear, for all the hurt I've caused you.'

There was a lump in her throat that would have choked her if she had tried to speak.

So this was the way it would end, she thought, and was conscious of an illogical feeling of relief. At least now she could stop fighting! The thing she had most dreaded had happened, and she could stop worrying about when it might strike her down.

Drew sat down on the arm of her chair, his big hand gentle against the softness of her hair.

Suddenly she could stay calm no longer. She pushed his hand away with a sudden strength that surprised her, and jumped up from her chair. 'I can't stand it,' she stormed. 'I can't take another instant of this!' Suddenly sobs overtook her, tearing at her throat, threatening to choke her. She fled through the drawing room and up the stairs, and slammed her bedroom door behind her.

Her room was still and cool. She flung herself across her bed and wept till her pillow was soaked, more tears than she had thought it possible for one person to shed. It was over. Too late, she had discovered what he meant to her, and now he was gone from her.

No, she told herself, and sniffled, that wasn't strictly true. He had always belonged to Cynthia; any thoughts that Brodie had cherished in these last few days that he might someday come to love her had been only romantic wishes. It had been a hopeless situation from the first, and Cynthia had been right. It would be better for both of them to make the break, to get a new start.

Her sobs died slowly and she lay still, clutching the wet pillow, her throat aching. She heard the door open, but she was too exhausted to protest.

'Brodie?' He sounded worried.

'Go away!' Her voice was only a croak.

'I will not touch you again. I swear it.'

She had no strength to fight him, but the tears started to slide down her face again as he sat down in the rocking chair next to her bed.

'Don't cry, darling,' he said. 'Please don't cry.' His voice was so gentle that she wanted to drown in it. It was the way he used to speak to her when she was ill, and it brought back all the easy memories of the days when she had been confident that he cared about her.

Loving someone is hard, she thought. I wonder whether this awful ache in my chest is what it feels like when a heart breaks.

'I did tell you, I believe, that if it was your wish I would set you free. Is that what you want?'

How she would have laughed, that day when his promise had been made, if someone had told her that she would bitterly regret it! She gulped and nodded.

He sighed. 'Brodie, I owe you a debt of gratitude. A lot of things have become clear to me this summer.'

Cynthia being chief among them. Brodie thought.

'I want us to stay friends, Bro.'

'I don't want to be your friend,' she choked.

He seemed to flinch. Then he sighed and said, 'I am grateful for your patience in the last few weeks.'

Brodie could take no more. If he tells me about how much he loves Cynthia, she thought, I will just start screaming.

She whispered, hoarsely, 'Don't say anything more,

please,' She swallowed hard. 'It's a dreadful thing to love someone and not be able to have him.'

There was an instant of silence, and then he said, his voice hard, 'You won't have much longer to wait for Jerry. I doubt he'll contest Isabel's divorce, so in a matter of weeks you'll be able to take up your hobby of reforming him.'

His voice was like a lash, and she struck back. 'I still don't have any money. I have nothing to offer Jerry, remember?'

'Oh, Oliver will have to pay him off. The prenuptial agreement was a generous one. In fact, if I didn't know Jerry so well, I'd wonder if he hadn't beaten Isabel up on purpose—so he could get rid of her and still have the money. But I'm sure he wouldn't be contented with so little, when he could have it all. And of course you won't come out of this marriage exactly penniless, Brodie.' His voice was sharp with sarcasm. 'Between the two of you, I'm certain you'll be able to keep the wolf from the door.'

She gasped. 'As if I'd take your money——'

'Why shouldn't you? You've earned it.'

She stared straight at him. 'What about my trust fund, Drew?'

His voice cracked like a whip. 'Who told you about that?'

'Does it matter?'

'No.' He ran a hand through his hair. 'You're right, Brodie. We might as well put all the cards on the table, while we're at it. You certainly know what you're getting if you marry Jerry—you might as well know what you'll be handing over to him, as well.'

'There really is a trust fund?' she whispered.

'Oh, yes. Andy wanted you to be well taken care of.' His voice was dry. 'So he put a great deal of his life insurance into trust for you. He didn't stop to think that he was making you a prime target for the Jerry's of this world.'

'Why wasn't I ever told?'

'I didn't want you to know. The expectation of coming into money does nasty things to kids sometimes. I'd intended to tell you this summer—start teaching you how to handle it.'

Brodie hardly heard. 'But you told Jerry that I wouldn't get anything——'

'I told him,' Drew corrected grimly, 'that your father didn't leave you a cent. Which is literally true. He didn't ask me if my father had done anything for you, so I didn't tell him. And then I prayed that you wouldn't find out, or you'd have gone running straight back to him. As you probably will now.'

Drew hadn't lied after all, she thought with a sudden wave of relief. She sat up on the bed. 'How much money is there?' she asked softly.

He looked as if he would like to tear her to pieces. 'Of course that would be your first question,' he said bitterly. 'Half a million, give or take. Plenty to take care of the two of you, even with Jerry's no doubt expensive tastes.'

'That's a lot of money,' Brodie breathed.

'It grows, over twelve years, when it sits idle.' He stood up, as if the chair was too confining, and started to pace the floor. 'I wish to hell I had used it—every penny of it. At least I could have kept you safe from Jerry, then. Instead, I had to be noble and protect your future——'

'You didn't use it?' she whispered.

'I never touched it, dammit. I wanted to take care of you, Brodie. You were precious to me, and I wanted to provide for you myself.' His jaw tensed. 'But if you're so damned dumb that you're ready to walk into that trap again, knowing what he is and what he did to Isabel, then I'm finished, Brodie!' He was almost shouting. 'Don't come crying to me when he beats you up.'

'I'm not that crazy.' He didn't seem to hear her. It

was probably better that way, she thought. She only hoped that he would never realise that she was free of Jerry only because she had fallen in love with Drew.

'I've half a mind to fight your damned divorce, Brodie. Maybe someday you'll come to your senses, if I can only wait long enough.' He clenched his fist, and slammed it into his other hand. Frustration was written deep into his face.

'You would only be punishing yourself.' She slid off the bed and walked over to the windows, staring out over the little town.

'There was a time when I thought we might have a chance,' he mused. 'Why did you come to me that night, Brodie?' Very slowly, he advanced across the room towards her.

'It doesn't matter now,' she whispered, and retreated.

'What went wrong that night, my dear?' His voice was low, but there was a command in it that she could not deny.

She moistened her lips and backed a little farther away from him. 'Pretending wasn't good enough, Drew.'

'I see,' he said. 'You couldn't forget that I wasn't Jerry, is that it?'

I didn't try to forget you. The words echoed inside her head, and for an instant Brodie was afraid she had actually said them. 'No, I couldn't,' she whispered. I couldn't ignore the fact that you don't love me, Drew, she thought.

'Did you do it to get even with him?' Drew mused. 'To pay him back for what he'd done to you?'

She shook her head.

'Or did you intend to throw off my suspicions? Make me believe that you weren't having an affair with him?'

Her hands were clenched on the back of a chair. 'No,' she said, and her voice cracked. 'Don't cheapen it——'

'I see,' he said quietly. 'And now you want to be free so you can go to Jerry.'

It would be so easy to nod, to let him go on believing that, to protect herself from the pain that would come if he suspected the truth. And yet the thread of steel in his voice would not permit her to lie to him.

'Don't do it, Brodie,' he said. 'To go back to Jerry—You can't be that stupid!'

'You dare to say that to me!' she exploded. She turned on him like a wildcat. 'You dare call me stupid! You're the one who's ready to——' She broke off with a sob.

'What am I supposedly ready to do?'

She shook her head. 'It doesn't matter,' she whispered.

'And you want a divorce.' He was so close to her that his breath was warm against her cheek. There was no place left for her to run to.

'I want out,' she said. The words seemed to stick in her throat. 'I don't care about the trust fund or a divorce settlement or anything. I just want out, Drew!'

'Brodie—look at me.' There was a note in his voice that was almost a plea for her to be sensible.

She shook her head again, and then pulled away from him as he tried to force her to raise her face. 'Don't touch me,' she said, and backed away.

'Are you afraid of me?'

Yes, she thought. I'm afraid that if you put a hand on me that I'll crack and beg you to make love to me and not to leave me ever again.

'Brodie,' he said, and his voice was full of pain, 'I tried never to hurt you.'

She blinked tears away. 'But you have,' she said. 'You've hurt me so much—My life is in shreds because of you!'

He flinched as if she had slapped him.

'I'm tired of fighting!' she cried. Her fists were clenched so tight that her nails cut into the palms. 'Go away, Drew. Go to Cynthia. That's what you want, so why play these awful games any more?'

'What if I don't want Cynthia?' he said quietly.

'Don't lie to me!' She was almost screaming. 'You told her about Jerry—and that you married me so she wouldn't suspect you still loved her.'

There was a moment of silence. Then he said thoughtfully, 'Fascinating.'

'You can't deny it—it's true. You knew she was coming back. You must have known.'

'Yes, I knew.'

'I don't blame you, but I wish you'd been honest! If you'd told me——' She stopped and took a deep breath, then went on doggedly. 'You'll be miserable with Cynthia, and if you'd only stop and look you could see that. Eric is a brat, and she's a liar and a schemer——'

There was a moment of frozen silence. Then Drew said, with an odd note in his voice, 'Would it matter to you if I was miserable?'

She shook her head defiantly, her long hair swinging, hiding her eyes. 'I don't care what you do. It's your life. Ruin it any way you please.'

He was silent for a long time. He was so close to her that she could almost feel his heartbeat. Then he sighed heavily and said, 'Very well, Brodie. I haven't much left to lose——' His hand closed on her chin and forced her to look up at him.

'What are you doing?' she protested.

'This is just one last, simple thing. You want to be free? Very well. I'm going to kiss you goodbye.'

'No.' She was breathless with foreboding.

'It's a small thing to ask—a kiss, that's all,' he mused, as if talking to himself.

It was little enough, she had to admit, if that was the price of her freedom. And surely it wasn't wrong to be in his arms one last time, to share one precious moment that would have to keep her warm through all the years to come—the lonely years when he would belong to Cynthia, and Brodie would be alone.

She looked up into his slate-green eyes, and held her

breath, almost hypnotised by the fire she saw there. Very slowly, he bent his head till his mouth brushed hers.

The feather-light contact was like a surge of electric current through Brodie's body. She shivered and, unable to prevent herself from responding, let her hands slip slowly through his dark hair to clasp at the back of his neck.

A light flared in Drew's eyes at her surrender, and the next kiss was neither gentle nor hesitant. He pulled her closer till her body was moulded against the hard strength of his. The pressure of his lips demanded her response, and she scarcely noticed as his hand slid under her blouse, unhesitatingly finding and caressing her breast.

'Did kissing Jerry ever make you feel like this?' he demanded huskily.

Brodie shook her head.

'Are you going back to him?'

'No.' It was a hoarse croak.

He smiled then, satisfied, and set about kissing her with slow, patient sensuousness. When his arms relaxed, Brodie swayed back against the wall, her eyes closed. Already she regretted that she had let him kiss her. It could make things harder. Without that kiss, she might have been able to convince herself that their single night together had been nothing unusual. Now, she thought, her mind still fuzzy from the sensations he had evoked, she could fool herself no longer. And the admission he had just forced from her—what was it she had said?

But it was important to pull herself together, so that he could not see the damage he had caused. She forced her eyes to open. 'Goodbye, Drew,' she said, very softly.

'Oh, no, little one,' he whispered against her lips. 'You're not getting away now.'

'Just a kiss, you said, and then I could go——'

He shrugged. 'So I didn't tell the truth. And besides,

that could hardly be called an ordinary kiss. It was more like nitroglycerine, if you ask me.' His voice was muffled; he was nibbling her earlobe.

'Please . . .'

'That lovely little voice can lie. But your body can't, my dear.'

'You promised.'

'I'm only human. Don't expect me to be more. I want you.'

'Because you feel responsible for me.'

'At the moment I feel very irresponsible indeed.' He shifted his attention to her throat, nibbling his way down to the hollow where her pulse beat wildly against his mouth.

Her breath was coming unevenly, hurting her throat. Why was he torturing her like this?

'There are a lot of things I've been wondering about, Brodie.' His voice was light, conversational. If anyone had overheard him, Brodie thought dizzily, they'd have thought he was questioning a friendly witness in the courtroom.

'You called my name that night, warning me when Jerry would have hit me with the fruit bowl. Why?'

'Because I didn't want you to be hurt.' She tried to pull his hands away from her delicate skin, but he merely found new places to caress that brought her breath even faster. 'Would you stop?' she pleaded finally.

He raised his head for an instant, his eyes brilliant green. 'Never,' he said firmly, and kissed her again.

'Drew, stop this and talk to me. I can't think when you're kissing me!'

'That's the general idea.' Then he sighed and reluctantly released her. 'All right, Brodie. You're free. What do you want to talk about?'

She felt suddenly cold and alone, outside the comfort of his arms. 'Cynthia.'

'I'd rather talk about us.' Then he sighed. 'All right. I

have never said anything to Cynthia about you, or our marriage, or Jerry. Anything she knows she got from Daniel—who doesn't know much. Whatever she said is mostly speculation, coloured by your own guilty conscience until you convinced yourself that she knew what she was talking about.'

Could he be right? 'Did she break off your engagement years ago because of me?'

'No.' He looked down at her. 'Oh, it was because of you, all right. But she didn't break it off. I did.'

Brodie's head snapped up. 'You're joking.'

'Thank you, by the way. If it hadn't been for you, I'd probably have married her, sold Safe Harbour, moved East . . .'

'Sold Safe Harbour?' She was horrified.

'I didn't do it,' he said defensively. 'Don't yell at me. Now that we've disposed of Cynthia as a topic——'

'You kept all of her letters.'

'As a reminder of how lucky I'd been.'

'Why didn't you tell me?'

'Because I knew you wouldn't marry me if I told you the truth.'

'You said that you could never forget your first love.'

'That's true. I never shall, Brodie. You are my first, my only love, Cynthia was a boy's infatuation, and over the years I've felt nothing for her so much as relief that I didn't marry her.' He looked down at her with a raised eyebrow, as if expecting a response.

'That's how I feel about Jerry,' she admitted softly.

'Then it's all settled.' The warmth in his eyes was like a sensual hand stroking her.

She fought it off. 'What is settled?' Her head was spinning, and suddenly she didn't know what she wanted.

'If you've finally realised that you don't want Jerry any more——'

'That doesn't necessarily mean that I want you.' She didn't even hear how harsh the words were until she saw him wince. She tried to soften the blow. 'Drew, you've always made my decisions for me. Isn't it time I started doing that for myself?'

He ran an unsteady hand through his hair. 'Please, Bro . . .'

'I need a few minutes to think,' she said quietly. 'This is so sudden . . .'

She left him there, in her room, and wandered through the house and out to the gardens. Raindrops still hung on the last of the full-blown iris; the storm had shattered some of the mature flowers and strewn petals over the lawn. She brushed against a shrub and water cascaded down the leg of her jeans.

Can I believe him? The question nagged at her. For so long, she had accepted unquestioningly that he loved Cynthia. It was hard to believe that she might have been wrong, that his love might have died, as he said it had.

Yours did, she reminded herself. You were infatuated with Jerry, and when that burned itself out, you saw what had been underneath all along—a fierce need for Drew.

But why would Drew need me, she wondered, and bit her lip. Was it that old monster, responsibility, raising its head again?

There was the trust fund, she reminded herself. Drew hadn't been forced to complicate his life by marrying her; she would be provided for, no matter what he did.

She looked up, and saw him in the doorway, standing with one hand braced high on the brick wall, watching her. There was no courtroom hush in his face now; from across the garden she could see the emotions warring. It's fear, she thought. He's actually afraid that I'll leave.

The last doubt in the corner of her mind burned up, leaving not even a cinder remaining, and she started to run, not bothering to skirt puddles. He met her on the flagstone steps at the edge of the garden, and she flung herself into his arms with a force that staggered him for an instant.

'I had to be certain,' she said breathlessly. 'I could have made another mistake so easily—'

'This is no mistake.' His arms tightened, and he lifted her off her feet to kiss her.

'The neighbours will see,' she breathed.

'If this sort of thing shocks them, they'd better start looking for a new house,' Drew threatened. 'Because they're apt to see a lot of it in the future.'

'I can't promise you a comfortable marriage with no emotional storms.'

'Good.'

'Why didn't you tell me the truth?'

'What could I tell you? That I wanted to make love to you so much that it tore me up to pass your room at night? That I wanted you so badly that I was afraid of what I'd do?' His voice was harsh with remembered pain.

'How long have you known?' she whispered.

'I think I've always known. But all I could do was wait, and hope that someday you'd fall in love with me instead of that poor excuse for a man.' He gave her a little shake.

Brodie giggled. 'Is that why you punched Jerry?'

'It was the single most satisfying moment of my life. No—there are a few others that were even better.' There was a teasing gleam in his eyes that brought hot colour to her face. Then he sobered. 'Bro—it would have killed me to give you away.'

'I'm glad,' she whispered, and there was no trace of laughter left in her voice. 'I love you, Drew. You're right about Safe Harbour. It's not the house. I've always felt protected here because of you.'

He brushed a drop of rainwater out of her hair. 'Let's go dry you out before you catch cold,' he said. 'It wouldn't be too much of a honeymoon to have you come down with pneumonia.'

'In sickness and in health, remember?' she teased.

'No matter what, my love,' he said, and the tone of his voice was a promise so powerful that Brodie shivered with happiness.

As they went inside, hand in hand, Safe Harbour seemed to settle down gently around them with a comfortable sigh.

*Shay Flanagan is Gypsy,
the raven-haired beauty who inflamed passion
in the hearts of two Falconer men.*

Carole Mortimer

GYPSY

Lyon Falconer, a law unto himself, claimed Shay—when
he didn't have the right. Ricky Falconer, gentle and loving
married Shay—when she had no other choice.

Now her husband's death brings Shay back within Lyon's
grasp. Once and for all Lyon intends to prove that Shay
has always been—will always be—*his* Gypsy!

Take 4 best-selling love stories FREE
Plus get a FREE surprise gift!

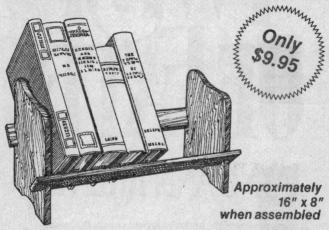

One of America's best-selling romance authors writes
her most thrilling novel!

TWIST OF FATE

JAYNE ANN KRENTZ

Hannah inherited the anthropological papers that could
bring her instant fame. But will she risk her life and give
up the man she loves to follow the family tradition?